ENTER A LOVER

ENTER A LOVER

Juliet Gray

Chivers Press • **Thorndike Press**
Bath, England **Waterville, Maine USA**

This Large Print edition is published by Chivers Press, England, and by Thorndike Press, USA.

Published in 2002 in the U.K. by arrangement with the author.

Published in 2002 in the U.S. by arrangement with Juliet Burton Literary Agency.

U.K. Hardcover ISBN 0–7540–4835–7 (Chivers Large Print)
U.S. Softcover   ISBN 0–7862–3942–5 (Nightingale Series Edition)

The text of this Large Print edition is unabridged.
Other aspects of the book may vary from the original edition.

Set in 16 pt. New Times Roman.

Printed in Great Britain on acid-free paper.

British Library Cataloguing in Publication Data available

Library of Congress Cataloging-in-Publication Data

Gray, Juliet.
     Enter a lover / Juliet Gray.
        p. cm.
     ISBN 0–7862–3942–5 (lg. print : sc : alk. paper)
     1. Large type books. I. Title.
     PR6057.R3268 E57 2002
     823'.914—dc21   2001058475

CHAPTER ONE

Miranda was bored.

She sipped her wine and smiled, pretending interest, while Jeremy droned on about a particularly clever business deal he had just pulled off, and wondered why she wasted her time in his company. He was a good-looking bore, she thought wryly. Very wealthy, very well-connected, very presentable—and a bore. She wondered if she could plead a headache and bring the weary evening to an early end.

It had been past midnight when they reached this expensive and very exclusive club where the in people liked to dance until dawn. It was the kind of place that Miranda liked to visit—in the right company. But Jeremy talked too much and did not dance well and his good looks and wealth and the notice that attached to being seen with him did not compensate for his dullness.

She stifled a little yawn. 'Let's dance,' she said, breaking into his monologue.

Jeremy was slightly pained, having just reached the most telling point of his story. But he was a well-mannered man and he rose instantly. 'Of course . . .! I'm afraid I'm boring you, darling. I'm sorry!' She was very beautiful and he loved her and he was anxious that she should enjoy the evening with him.

Miranda slipped into his arms. He was a poor dancer but anything was better than his conversation, she thought impatiently, wondering again why she encouraged him. His attraction for her had been very short-lived.

The dance floor was small, known as intimate, and very crowded. Jeremy held her much too tightly, possessively. As they moved to the music Miranda kept him as much at bay as she could, abruptly disliking his ardour and his closeness. Over his shoulder, she met the dark eyes of a man who watched with amused interest from his vantage point at the bar. She felt a little shock of irritation as she recognised the mockery of his gaze. She looked away and refused to look again, oddly conscious that he willed her to do so.

She did not know him. She had never seen him before. Yet he was vaguely familiar and she wondered about him. He was not a tall man but he was impressive. Dark of hair and eye, burly of build without being overweight, he had the sensual good looks of the Jew. There was something striking about him, she thought—something that sent an odd little shiver down her spine as she found herself meeting his eyes once more. An attractive man but a dangerous one, she decided, feeling as if those glittering dark eyes looked straight into her soul.

He inclined his head in a nod of friendly recognition. Miranda frowned, knowing they

2

had never met. Her chin tilted just a fraction and she stared at him coldly, without interest. His mocking smile deepened. Then, quite pointedly, he turned his back to her and began to talk to one of the barmen. Instantly she was affronted and her eyes sparkled with indignation. Insolent devil, she thought angrily . . . and stumbled over Jeremy's feet.

He apologised at length and she lost patience with him. He was too nice, too well-meaning. A credit to his nanny, she thought drily—and not man enough for her! It was time they parted company.

They sat down and Miranda shook her head to the offer of more wine. 'Perhaps you should take me home,' she suggested hopefully. 'I'm in a foul mood. Nothing went right this evening. One of those nights we all dread in the business. Props went missing at the last minute, Harvey forgot his lines, the audience laughed in all the wrong places. Sheer disaster!'

'My poor darling,' he said gently. 'Of course I'll take you home.' He lifted her hand to his lips and smiled at her lovingly. 'You must be exhausted.'

She wanted to scream at him. He made her feel so guilty with his niceness, his patience. He was Edward all over again, she thought wearily.

'No. Just bad-tempered and taking it out on you,' she said frankly.

3

'I haven't noticed. You're always very sweet to me, Miranda. I love you very much,' he told her tenderly.

She withdrew her hand, none too gently. 'My dear Jeremy, you don't know me! I'm a bitch,' she declared impatiently. 'I expect your friends have already told you that I'm a shocking flirt and will most likely break your heart. Don't shake your head. It's true!'

'I'll risk it,' he said, smiling.

Miranda sighed. Clean-cut good looks and a healthy bank balance had always won him what he wanted. Just now, he wanted her. She would be wasting her breath if she tried to convince him that he was doomed to disappointment.

Jeremy gave a signal and the bill was brought to the table. He scrawled his name across it in a confident certainty that he was known and trusted. Miranda drew her wrap about her bare shoulders and rose to her feet. He ushered her through the tables with a protective, slightly possessive hand at her elbow and it took all her self-control not to shake it off in sudden dislike of being treated like a piece of porcelain . . .

A little smile flickered in Paul Keller's dark eyes as he watched their progress. He knew what she was thinking as definitely as if she had voiced it. Yet it was rare for a woman to resent such courteous attentiveness—and women usually liked the handsome Lord

Landon. He was intrigued by a woman who was so restive in the man's company.

He found her fascinating, exciting. She was very beautiful. Tall and very slender, very self-possessed, a woman to attract instant attention, instant admiration, instant desire. Paul was a sensual man and women were very necessary in his life. Suddenly he knew that he wanted the woman who walked towards him, wanted her very much. She refused to meet his eyes, he noticed, although he knew that she was very much aware of him. He caught his breath at her beauty, the superb lines of her body. She wore black, a delicate froth of layered chiffon that complemented the gleaming auburn hair and sapphire eyes and the delicate skin that went with such colouring.

He moved forward, smiling. 'How are you, Jeremy?'

Jeremy was genuinely pleased to see him. Miranda thought drily that he was like an eager puppy, delighted to be noticed. She would have walked on but Jeremy was anxious to introduce her to his friend.

'Miranda, may I introduce Paul Keller. Paul . . . Miranda Lynch. She's an actress, you know.'

He clasped the slim, slightly reluctant hand and smiled into the unsmiling eyes. 'I do know, of course,' he said lightly. 'I may tell you that I sat through an abominable excuse for entertainment at the *Zeus* because your

5

presence in the cast redeemed an otherwise wasted evening.'

'You must be a critic, Mr. Keller,' she said with tart sweetness. 'You know all the right words.' She had been a little shaken to discover his identity. Everyone had heard of Paul Keller, nightclub owner, notorious rake and gambler, near-criminal with his finger in too many of Soho's suspicious pies. She had been right to think of him as dangerous, she realised. He was certainly not a man to tangle with . . . which made her all the more inclined to tangle with him, she thought with stirring excitement. He was very attractive and his dark eyes rested on her with unmistakable admiration. Her pulses quickened slightly. Most men were very unexciting. Paul Keller looked as though he would be a very exciting man to know . . .

'The critics didn't use them,' he reminded her drily. 'They praised the play.' He turned to Jeremy. 'Can I persuade you and Miss Lynch to have a drink with me?'

'That's very nice of you, Paul. But Miranda is a little tired. I'm just about to take her home.' He was warm and friendly and eager to please. But he was not entirely a fool and he sensed the instant rapport between them . . . and he did not mean to give the spark an opportunity to burst into flame. Paul was a friend but his reputation with women was too well-known. And Jeremy was in love with

Miranda and did not want to lose her.

He was relieved that she did not speak of the man as they drove through almost deserted streets to the block of luxury flats where she lived. It did not occur to him that it would have been less suspicious if she had shown interest in his friendship with someone who was seldom out of the public eye for long.

In fact, Miranda scarcely spoke at all. And Jeremy, genuinely concerned, fancied that she was very tired and felt that it had been selfish to expect her to spend half the night at the popular *Hobo Club* in his company. When they arrived at Seal Court, she did not invite him in for a nightcap and he swallowed his disappointment. Reluctantly she allowed him to kiss her but her lips were cool, offputting. Jeremy was quick to make allowances for her coldness.

'Lunch with me tomorrow, darling?' he suggested. 'Somewhere quiet and rather nice . . . I know just the place.'

Miranda shook her head. 'No. I mean to have a really lazy day tomorrow, Jeremy. I need to unwind. Life has been a little too hectic lately.' She touched her fingers to his smooth cheek in a careless caress. 'Goodnight, my dear . . .'

He escorted her to the lift despite her assurance that it was unnecessary. Taking her hand, he lifted it to his lips, smiling down at her with devotion. 'Then I'll see you tomorrow night after the performance. I'll be waiting to take you home—or wherever you wish to go.'

Miranda glanced at him with a little frown in her lovely eyes, disliking the note in his voice which implied that he was beginning to take the initiative in their relationship. She had obviously encouraged him too much! 'You mustn't try to monopolise me, Jeremy,' she said lightly but with a meaning he could not mistake. 'I do have other friends, you know. Ring me on Thursday and we'll arrange something.' She stepped into the lift and smiled brightly and without real warmth as the doors slid across, unaffected by the disappointment in his expression.

Utterly indifferent to his feeling for her and attaching very little importance to it, Miranda dismissed him immediately.

She let herself into the flat that she had taken over from a girl who had returned to America at a very convenient time for Miranda. For the opportunity had offered just as Miranda decided to put an end to the affair à la Edward and needed a new roof over her head.

She tossed her wrap on a chair, kicked off her shoes and sank onto the sofa with her feet up. She did not feel at all like going tamely to bed. She was not tired. She was all keyed up, in fact . . . just as though she expected something to happen at any moment. And that was absurd. For few of her friends would call at one o'clock in the morning.

Her heart was racing and she felt oddly breathless. She was restless, too . . . a little fever in her blood hankering for the strength of a man's arms about her and the passion in his kiss, the promise and the fulfilment of ecstacy. In her mind's eye, she saw again the dark, mocking eyes, the sensual mouth with its hint of cruelty, the handsome face of a dangerously attractive man—and she understood her impatience with the well-meaning geniality of men like Jeremy. She attracted nice men, she thought wryly—and invariably hurt them! For they were too nice, lacking some quality that added a certain spice to life. Paul Keller possessed that quality in full measure, she sensed. She wondered when she would see him again. It was not a question of 'if'. She knew that something had sparked between them . . . and it was the reason for her inner excitement.

She had been in and out of love a dozen times since her early teens. She had fallen in love at first sight with Edward. She knew about loving and her own inability to love for long. This feeling that Paul Keller excited had nothing to do with love. She was mature enough to face facts. She wanted him in exactly the same way that he wanted her. There was no point in dressing it up in fancy frills, she told herself firmly. Then no one was disappointed when the flame burned itself out

9

as it inevitably would.

As it had with Edward . . .

He was a talented and very successful actor and they had met at a theatre in the Strand. He had a leading part in a new play and Miranda had gone along to audition with several other girls for the part of the 'other woman'. She had got the part and Edward had taken her to lunch. They had still been together the next morning. She had been swept off her feet by his blond good looks, his charm and self-assurance, the very niceness of the man.

They had been very much in love and it was a joyous affair for some time. Edward had assumed a happy ending. But Miranda had refused to be rushed into marriage just when she had secured an important part that would demand a great deal of her attention and energy. Edward, equally dedicated to his work, had understood. However, being an optimist, he had bought a small, cleverly modernised Victorian cottage in Harrow, just down the hill from the school, and set about making it home for them both.

Miranda, loving him, had moved in with him. Yet loving him did not reconcile her to the prospect of marriage. She had little or no faith in marriage. She was not even sure that love could last forever but it seemed likely to last a lot longer without the restricting bonds of matrimony.

The play had run for some months. When it came off, Edward had tried to persuade her to marry him. They had quarrelled and made up and quarrelled again. He would not accept her point of view. He could not understand her resistance to being tied down. He had pointed out that loving was a tie in itself and that marriage was only one step beyond living together. Miranda had told him firmly that it was a step she did not mean to take. She had to be free!

Eventually Edward had accused her of no longer loving him . . . and she had agreed, a little sadly. She had fallen out of love as swiftly as she had fallen into it, she admitted with the honesty that was so much a part of her character. It was time to part, to accept that they had made a mistake.

He had refused to accept—and he was still refusing, still clinging to the belief that she loved him and would return to him. He still insisted that they were right for each other and declared that she would never find real happiness with any other man. For himself, he felt no desire even to look at another woman!

It was very flattering. But it irked Miranda who had never wanted to be responsible for anyone else's happiness or peace of mind. No one could love or not love to order, of course. But she felt it was a weakness on Edward's part to go on caring, to have so little pride or self-respect. He had been badly hurt but it was some weeks since she had left him and he ought to be getting over it by now.

He wrote long, loving letters that she found too painful to read. He telephoned her frequently. Occasionally he persuaded her to meet him for a meal or a drink and always he broke his promise not to talk of the past or try to involve her in his future.

Miranda did not know why all her feeling for him had so suddenly fled. Very often, she regretted it. Edward was a dear, a good and generous man that everyone liked, and he had done his utmost to make her happy during the months that they had been together. He was the kind of man that any woman ought to find easy to love—and she had loved him in those first blissful months. But she did not love him now . . . and that proved how wise she had been to obey her instinct and refuse to marry him.

Now she was tingling all over with an excitement born of a brief encounter with another man . . . and wouldn't her reaction have been exactly the same if she had been married to Edward? Which surely proved that she was simply not the type of woman who could commit herself wholeheartedly for the rest of her life to one man . . .

She rose impatiently from the sofa. What on earth was she waiting for? A telephone call? A ring at the doorbell? Paul Keller did not even know where she lived! She must allow him time to gather the information . . .

CHAPTER TWO

Miranda did not sleep very well. Waking or sleeping, her thoughts kept revolving around a man she did not know and would certainly be a fool to trust. Just as she was thinking about getting up, the sun high in the sky, she fell into a deep sleep—and was startled awake by the strident summons of the telephone beside her bed.

She lay still, allowing it to ring for a full minute. Then, leisurely, a confident little smile hovering about her lips, she reached for the receiver.

It was Edward and disappointment swept over her in waves. She fancied he could hear it in her voice but it was rather too late to consider his feelings, she thought wryly.

'Is anything wrong?' he asked gently, swiftly sensitive to her mood.

'I was asleep.'

'Late night?'

'Why are you ringing at this unearthly hour, Edward?' she demanded lightly, ignoring the question. He would not want to know that she had been out with Jeremy Landon or any other man.

He laughed. 'It's eleven o'clock! I didn't dare to disturb you earlier although I'm bursting with news. Listen, darling! That part

13

in the new Agatha Christie film . . . it's mine! We begin shooting in the autumn—on location in Cairo! What do you think about that? It's only a small part, as I told you, but it is an important one.'

'Great!' She tried to be thrilled for him but Edward's affairs seemed to be very remote from her own concerns these days. 'That's really marvellous. I'm so pleased, Edward.' She stifled a yawn and discovered she was hungry. Edward had been marvellous about bringing her breakfast on a tray after a late night. He had spoiled her, of course. A tender, loving man, she thought on a surge of affection. Sometimes she missed him very much.

He was full of his news and she listened dutifully, murmuring the right words in the right places, visualising him as he talked. He would be sprawled full length on the sofa, telephone tucked into his shoulder, a tall, lean, very good-looking man with his blond hair boyishly tousled at this moment, no doubt. His blue eyes would be eager with delight and his very attractive smile coming and going as he talked. He was very endearing. She had known a great deal of happiness with him, she remembered. Strange that it should have evaporated so abruptly . . .

'But I'm telling it all now!' he suddenly exclaimed. 'Miranda, we have to celebrate! You'll meet me for a drink tonight after the curtain falls, won't you? I can't make it before. I'll be tied up with agents and press and what-have-you and I'm working tonight. You know more than anyone what this means to me—and I know you care more than anyone. Please, Miranda!'

Sentiment still lingering, she weakly agreed . . . and regretted the arrangement as soon as she replaced the receiver. It was not a good idea to meet Edward. He loved her too much and expected too much and never gave up hope that she would go back to him. It was quite impossible. She could never belong so utterly to any man as Edward demanded. She needed her freedom . . .

Miranda uttered the last lines and the curtain slowly descended to a very faint round of applause. She exchanged a wry glance with Harvey Reed, her co-star. She knew as well as he did that the play could not last many more nights. They were playing to almost empty houses and no amount of alteration to script or 'business' could resuscitate something that had virtually died on the first night. The play was a comedy of manners in eighteenth-century style and simply lacked popular appeal.

She left the stage and went to her dressing-room. Polly Perry, a dresser for forty years who liked to reminisce about the old days, helped her out of the close-fitting period costume and handed her a silk kimono. Miranda knotted the robe about her slender waist and sat down before the mirror to remove the stage make-up.

She had plenty of time before meeting Edward who was currently appearing at the National Theatre as Orlando in a modern-day version of *As You Like It* and apparently giving a superb performance. He was a very good actor and had been described more than once as a young Olivier. The curtain did not come down at the National for another half-hour and she must allow Edward time to change and cross the river to the small pub in the Strand where they had arranged their rendezvous.

With a part of her, she was looking forward to seeing him. She was really very fond of Edward and she was glad that their parting had not meant the absolute end of everything between them. Miranda liked to keep her friends. At the same time, it was scarcely fair to encourage him to go on hoping that she might change her mind . . . and it was encouragement if she only met him for a friendly drink from time to time. It was very difficult to know what to do for the best, she thought wryly.

She disliked wigs and her own hair was carefully dressed and powdered for each night's performance by the skilful Polly. The talkative little woman was brushing the powder from the long, thick ringlets and describing at some length her days with a famous actress of the past who could actually sit on her thick auburn hair when someone rapped peremptorily on the door.

'Come . . .!' Miranda called carelessly, expecting Harvey or another member of the cast to enter for a drink or a chat about the play.

The door opened and her heart missed a beat as she saw Paul Keller framed in the opening, reflected in the big mirror of her dressing-table. She was startled and yet not at all surprised to see him. Meeting his eyes in the mirror and abruptly aware of a little glow in their depths that was already becoming familiar, her pulses quickened. She turned.

He smiled and bowed slightly with unexpected and faintly foreign courtesy. 'Good evening.'

'Mr. Keller, isn't it?' She raised an eyebrow in cool query.

His smile deepened. 'Just as you expected,' he said mockingly.

She felt a touch of confusion. It was disconcerting that any man should read her thoughts so easily. Then she laughed and held out a hand to him. 'Just as I expected,' she agreed with a frankness to match his own. She nodded to the hovering Polly. 'I can manage now, Polly . . . thanks very much.'

The little woman reluctantly went away, having recognised Miranda's caller and wondering what he could want with a nice young woman who ought to know better than to encourage a man with his reputation.

Paul took her slender hand and held it in both his own, looking down at her . . . and he sensed the ripple of excitement at his touch and his own desire quickened. She was beautiful . . . and she was passionate. She was a woman that he wanted very much. 'You were magnificent,' he said softly. 'But such a terrible setting for a beautiful jewel! We must find a play for you that doesn't empty the theatre despite your talent and your beauty.'

'You were out front . . . ?' Her heart lifted at the promise in his words but she did not allow him to think that they impressed her unduly.

He grimaced. 'One of the very few. Yes, my dear. I sat through it all again for the delight of watching you move and hearing you speak—and greater love hath no man . . .'

She looked at him doubtfully, cynicism in her sapphire eyes. 'You aren't a man to waste an evening without . . . without good reason, I suspect,' she said bluntly. She withdrew her hand from his warm clasp and picked up the hairbrush that Polly had laid down. She was glad to be occupied so that their eyes need not meet too often. Those dark eyes were disturbing, she found. There was that glow in their depths that excited even while it alarmed her just a little. He was a man of strong passions and it would not be wise to play

18

games with him, she felt.

'Without hope of reward, you began to say, I suspect,' he countered smoothly, amusement glinting in his eyes. 'You are right, of course. You will reward me by having supper with me.'

She glanced at him quickly. 'That's a little high-handed, isn't it?'

'Yes,' he agreed. He lifted a thick tress of her auburn hair in his hand, let it fall through his fingers in a gleaming cascade. 'You are a very lovely woman and a man must make his own opportunities,' he said deliberately. 'You are at liberty to refuse, of course.'

Miranda suddenly knew that no woman had ever said nay to him . . . and she was just as weak as all the others where he was concerned. He was a stranger and she ought not to trust him. Her instinct told her that he would take her and use her quite ruthlessly and discard her when it suited him. He was that kind of man. It would be absolute folly to encourage him, to become involved with him. Yet it did not even occur to her to hesitate, to think twice. The look in his eyes was enchantment, the touch of his hand was magic. After all, he was *her* kind of man . . .

'You have a lot to offer and a woman must make the most of her opportunities,' she returned lightly. 'I've no intention of refusing your kind invitation.' She saw something flicker in his face and fancied she had scored a point.

19

Paul was intrigued. He was not used to reproof, however gentle. It amused him. At the same time, her words caused him to wonder if he had been a little too high-handed, a little too arrogantly sure of her response.

He knew she was attracted. And she was forthright . . . a rare thing in a woman. Their affair—and he did not doubt that there was to be an affair—would be exciting, enjoyable and without lasting commitment. She would not pretend to love him like so many other women . . . and he need not pretend that she meant more than any of the women who had preceded her. They would both know exactly where they stood. His instinct had not let him down, he thought with satisfaction. After all, she *was* his kind of woman . . .

He bent suddenly and kissed her lips. A swift, fierce kiss that seemed to stamp her with his brand. Miranda was shaken, trembling. He had claimed her with that kiss . . . and abruptly she was not so sure that she wanted to belong to him, even briefly. She wanted him desperately—but what would it cost her in the long run?

Paul moved towards the door. 'I'll leave you to dress. My car will be outside the stage door in ten minutes.'

As the door closed, Miranda put down the hairbrush and frowned at her reflection in the mirror. Was she mad—or bewitched? Her mouth throbbed from that brief, almost bruising kiss and her heart was tumultuous in her breast. He was infuriatingly arrogant, commanding and demanding as the mood took him . . . so why did she not resent it? Why did she thrill to that masterful manner when she had always been so insistent on being her own mistress?

She had thought about Paul Keller half the night and throughout the day, *knowing* in the very heart of her that he would follow up the brief encounter of the previous night. So she had been unsurprised to see him in the doorway of her dressing-room. Delighted, thrilled, excited—and unsurprised. He had stepped out of the wings and on to the stage of her life, his part ready and waiting for him. *Enter A Lover* . . . exactly on cue and word-perfect. And only time would tell if it meant success or disaster. As always, Miranda would give herself utterly to her part . . .

He had thrust all thought of Edward out of her mind. Now, as she began to dress, she remembered him. She could not meet him now. She could not let Paul slip through her fingers . . . and she knew instinctively that there would not be a second chance. He was proud . . . and there were too many other women who would leap at the opportunity he offered. She was sorry about Edward who would be disappointed when she did not turn up . . . but she would apologise when she saw him, she decided, and turned her attention to her hair. With deft, skilful fingers, she twisted the thick, gleaming mass into a neat chignon on the nape of her neck and secured it firmly with a handful of pins. With haste but with care, she applied street make-up, thrust things into the beige handbag that matched the filmy shirt and elegant high-heeled shoes, and caught up the jacket of her tailored suit. She was ready . . . but only just within the ten minutes, she thought—and wondered why she did not think it wise to keep him waiting. Probably because he would not wait, she decided wryly . . . and her chance would be lost!

The engine was running, indication of his impatience. He leaned across to push open the passenger door of the white Rolls Royce. 'Get in.'

She hesitated and then got in beside him. 'Your manners are unusual,' she said lightly. 'Not good but unusual.'

He chuckled . . . a rich, throaty sound that was infectious. Suddenly liking him, Miranda smiled. He laid his hand briefly on her clasped fingers as they lay in her lap. 'You're a great girl,' he said warmly. 'I like you.'

She was pleased by the careless tribute as though he had paid her the highest compliment. But she did not betray her delight. 'I like you,' she returned drily. 'I wish I knew why.'

'Instant recognition of a kindred spirit,' he

22

said as the car glided from the kerb with a soft purr. 'Two of a kind—you and I. We speak the same language.'

'Body language,' she said bluntly . . . and wondered, not for the first time, if her insistence on honesty was an asset to a woman.

He nodded. 'That's right. It's good that you have no illusions. We can enjoy each other without guilt. That's important, isn't it?'

Everything in her leaped to agree with him. Loving between a man and a woman must be good indeed if there was absolute freedom on both sides, she felt. She recalled times in Edward's arms when she had yielded against instinct and without desire because he loved her and she was reluctant to hurt him . . . and been suffused with guilt because she could not love him, could not respond as he deserved. The need to ensure his delight and satisfaction had often inhibited her own pleasure in lovemaking and then, rather than hurt or disappoint or humiliate him, she had been forced to pretend . . . and hated herself for pretending. It was essential to Miranda to be honest, with herself and with other people— and it was a relief to meet someone as honest as herself. So she responded instinctively to the candour in this man's approach to their desire for each other which seemed so natural and inevitable.

At the same time, he must not cherish any false illusions about her. 'I'm not promiscuous,' she said abruptly. 'I'm no man's simply for the asking. Understand that, Paul Keller.'

'I'm not asking,' he said, smiling. 'I'm taking.'

Her chin tilted swiftly. 'You could be disappointed!'

'I believe in positive thinking,' he told her smoothly. 'A man who expects disappointment will be a loser all his life. You won't disappoint me.' He reached for her hand and carried it briefly to his lips.

'Where are we going?' she asked curiously, leaning forward in an attempt to identify their whereabouts. It seemed that they were rapidly leaving Theatreland and its environs behind them. 'I'm not dressed for clubbing,' she warned, indicating her white suit. He was wearing a midnight-blue dinner jacket with frilled dress shirt of powder-blue and formal bow tie and he looked handsome and very impressive.

'I see too much of clubs. We're having supper in my house. Everything's laid on.' He turned to look at her. 'Do you really suppose I want to share you with an audience on our first night?'

She knew a shock of desire at the quiet words, the look in his dark eyes. 'I think you take too much for granted,' she said slowly, wondering if he really expected her to melt into his arms at the lift of a finger—and if she had the strength to resist him at all.

He smiled. 'I think you leap to conclusions too quickly,' he countered smoothly. 'I'm not an Edward Kane to rush you into bed at the earliest opportunity. I hope I have more finesse.'

Miranda was startled. 'You know about Edward?'

'I made it my business to find out what men there are in your life,' he said coolly.

'Your business . . .' She frowned. 'I don't think I like that very much.' She felt chilled by the efficiency of his approach. Had he vetted her before deciding to follow up that initial attraction?

'You dislike knowing so little about me,' he told her, smiling.

'I know some bad things about you,' she returned swiftly.

He chuckled. 'You'll discover the good things as we go along.' He brought the car to a halt outside the tall, narrow, Georgian house that was situated in a well-known square in Belgravia. He was a man of means and liked to live well, to surround himself with beautiful things, to amuse himself with beautiful women. He had yet to come across something desirable that money could not buy . . .

CHAPTER THREE

Miranda was impressed by the discreet luxury of the house, its well-chosen furnishings, beautiful carpets, obviously valuable books and paintings and the exquisite porcelain that he liked to collect. He had taste as well as money, she thought with approval.

Supper was superbly cooked and efficiently served, accompanied by a wine that was deceptively light. He was an excellent host. They talked of the theatre . . . and also of books and music and art. Miranda was surprised to discover that he was very knowledgeable . . . much more so than herself.

After the meal, she relaxed in a deep, comfortable armchair while he sat at the piano and played for her. He was a sensitive and gifted musician, his fingers rippling across the keys, his concentration on the music proving that he played for pleasure rather than effect.

She studied him thoughtfully, interested as well as attracted by a man with unsuspected depths to his character and personality. She had thought him cold for all his obvious sensuality, calculating rather than instinctive, practical rather than imaginative. But he played Brahms and Schubert with warmth and sensitivity and imagination. Miranda, who loved music, warmed to the man who undoubtedly loved it too.

She rose and went to stand by him, watching the long, strong fingers as they unerringly sought the keys. He had powerful hands. She fancied that he knew how to take care of himself in a rough-house for all the sensitivity of his playing.

Paul had been lost in the music, almost forgetful of her presence. Suddenly aware of her, he ceased to play, turned towards her, drew her down to sit on the piano stool beside him. 'Now for your party piece,' he said, smiling.

Laughing, she began to play Chopsticks . . . and he joined her, his dark eyes glinting with amusement. Miranda found it ridiculously difficult to concentrate on playing the simple theme. She was so very conscious of his nearness, the latent passion that emanated from him, the very masculinity of the man that stirred her senses so strongly.

Their hands brushed. A little tremor rippled from the nape of her neck to the base of her spine. It was the oddest sensation and a little alarming, betraying her complete lack of resistance to his physical appeal. Had she no pride, no self-respect, no dignity that she was so ready to surrender to this stranger? It was odd that pride, self-respect, dignity all seemed to count for nothing in the face of the ecstacy she knew she would find in his arms.

Paul withdrew his hands from the keys. He

rose and reached for her, drawing her to her feet and into his embrace. Unsmiling, a nerve throbbing in his cheek, he looked down at her for a long, tense moment . . . and then he kissed her.

She was on fire at the first touch of his lips, helpless with wanting—and she wondered if it would always be like this and how she would bear it when he grew tired of her and turned away as a man like Paul Keller inevitably would. No man had ever moved her so, stirred her so swiftly to such desire . . . not even Edward in the days when she had loved him!

She uttered his name on a little sigh of longing. Paul swung her up and into his arms with ease and carried her to the long couch, laid her gently against the cushions. With warm invitation in her beautiful eyes, she put her arms about his neck and drew him down.

She was eager in his arms and her passion leaped to match his own. But Paul was not a man to rush his fences and a swift conquest was an easily forgotten one. Their affair was destined to be rather more memorable than most, he felt.

Miranda sensed the desire without the intent . . . and understood. He did not mean to take her with the careless, casual ease of his usual attitude to women. He was paying her the compliment of courtship after a fashion. She quietened in his arms, disappointed but docile, and found a different kind of delight in his kiss, his strong embrace, the slow caress of his hands on her body. He made gentle, undemanding love to her with the touch of an expert. She was surprised for everything about him hinted at fierce, primitive passion. She had not expected tenderness, the unselfish desire to give pleasure rather than take it for himself. He was a baffling, unexpected, unpredictable man . . .

He lay with his head on her breast, his lips warm on her soft flesh beneath the thin, unbuttoned shirt. Miranda teased the black curls that nestled on the nape of his neck . . . thick, springy, they leaped about her fingers with vital life.

'I must take you home,' he said abruptly, rearing his head. Comfortable, oddly content, he had been near to drowsing in her light embrace.

'Must you?' She met his eyes with direct appeal in her own. Suddenly she wanted to be taken to his bed on a swift storm of passion that ensured fulfilment, to sleep in his arms and to wake to his comforting nearness. She did not want to go back to her lonely bed.

He smiled . . . the slow glinting smile that held just a touch of disturbing mockery. 'The world doesn't end in the morning, Miranda. There will be other nights.'

'And other women!' she said before she could check the impulsive words.

He laughed. 'Possibly.' He rose and

stretched with lazy sensuality.

Miranda hated possessiveness. It was probably the one thing that had killed her love for Edward stone-dead. He had wanted to own her, body and soul. She did not and never would own Paul Keller. She did not wish to own him. She respected a man who remained his own master.

So she was horrified by the fierce flood of resentment that swept over her at the thought of him with another woman. There had been women before her, of course . . . too many! But that was the past. She wanted to be his present and his future! She wanted to be his woman so that all the world knew it and other women hesitated to cast out lures to him and Paul himself felt no need or desire or interest for other women.

'Other men, too,' she said lightly, as carelessly as she could. She swung her feet to the floor and searched for her shoes while her deft fingers were busy with the buttons of her shirt.

'Entirely as you wish,' he drawled. 'But not at the same time, Miranda. Me—*or* other men. Understood?'

'High-handed!' she exclaimed. She thrust her arms into the sleeves of her jacket. 'Can I expect the same of you?'

'Don't expect anything,' he said, smiling. 'I'm a perverse devil and might go out of my way to disappoint you.'

'I don't think I want you on those terms,' she said slowly, doubtfully.

He caught her to him swiftly, fiercely. 'Don't you?' he demanded, compelling her to meet his eyes with the very force of his personality. 'Don't you . . .?' He kissed her, long and lingering, rousing her to swift, breath-taking response.

Foolishly weak where he was concerned, she melted against him, clung to him, yielded to the enchantment in his kiss—and later, when he had driven off in his car to heaven knew where, leaving her with a painful abruptness, marvelled that any man should have such power to delight and disturb and dismay.

He was a strange man, she mused, letting herself into the flat. Any other man would have taken her without hesitation that night. She had shown herself more than willing. For reasons known only to himself, Paul Keller had treated her like a piece of the porcelain he valued so much . . . with a surprising tenderness, with an odd kind of respect. He was fascinating . . . and frustrating, she thought wryly. And wondered how she would get through the hours before she saw him again . . .

Whether it was the wine or the excitement or very little sleep, Miranda did not know. But she was stricken with migraine and spent a miserable day battling with it so she would be well enough for the evening performance. However bad the play or however small the audience, the show must go on, she thought wryly.

It did not help that she anticipated a call from Paul that did not come. She had fully expected him to ring her. He had left her without making arrangements to meet again but it had not seemed to matter. The rapport, the attraction, was too strong, she knew. But he did not call and she took a taxi to the theatre in a foul mood and with an aching head and that pitiless sickness at her stomach.

She struggled through the performance. Feeling quite ill, she hurried off stage as soon as the final curtain released her . . . and almost fell over Paul who was standing in the wings.

'Oh, it's you,' she said without warmth, wondering how he had contrived to sweeten George a second time. The old doorkeeper was usually very reliable in keeping strangers from trespassing backstage.

'You expected me to telephone,' he said with swift understanding.

'I haven't thought about you,' she said tartly and without truth, turning to walk along the corridor to her dressing-room.

'No more than I've thought about you,' he agreed smoothly. 'We are both busy people.'

She frowned slightly. 'What are you doing here? I won't believe that you've sat through the play a third time!'

'Not even for your sake,' he said with feeling. 'I've spent my evening with friends at

Covent Garden. No one will wonder at my missing the last act of my favourite opera. I'm known to be unpredictable.'

She paused with a hand on the door, unsmiling. 'Go back to your friends, Paul. I mean to go home as soon as I've changed and I'm in no mood for company.'

He saw the strain in her sapphire eyes, large and luminous in the pale oval of her lovely face. He bent to kiss her and she jerked from the touch of his lips.

Something very like anger leaped to his eyes and Miranda knew an odd little spasm of alarm. Did it matter so much that she did not alienate this man, she wondered in surprise.

'What's wrong?' he demanded with a hint of harshness.

She shook her head. 'I hate myself and everyone else tonight,' she told him wearily.

'Are you ill?'

'A migraine. I get them now and again. The best place for me is bed—as soon as possible and on my own!' The emphatic words made him chuckle but Miranda could not share his amusement. She bit her lips as another wave of sickness swept over her. She had never felt less attractive—and this was one man who must not see her at her worst! 'Oh, Paul—do go away!' she exclaimed, wretched.

Without another word, he turned. His footsteps echoed in the long corridor as he walked away from her. Looking after him,

Miranda knew she would desperately regret that rejection of him and felt too ill to care.

Polly fussed over her, insisting that she drank some sal volatile, brushing the powder from the thick hair with the gentlest of hands, assisting her to change with the minimum of movement.

'I know just how you feel, ducks,' she said with sympathy. 'I was exactly the same until I married my Henry. Cure for everything, marriage . . . including love if you ask me! There now! Your colour's coming back. I know the sal volatile is foul stuff but it's an old-fashioned remedy that *works*!'

'Yes. I shall be fine once I'm out of the theatre,' Miranda said, gritting her teeth. 'Thanks for everything, Polly . . . You're an angel.'

Without bothering to pin up her hair or put on street make-up, she made her way to the stage door. She managed a smile for old George. 'Do you think you could work a miracle and get me a taxi, George?' she asked, thankful that the crusty old curmudgeon had a weakness for a pretty face and a shapely leg.

'Your taxi's outside, miss . . . waiting for you,' he said with a nod and a wink.

Blessing Polly who had obviously had a word with him in advance, Miranda went out into the narrow street. She had not expected to find the white Rolls Royce standing at the kerb. She was even more surprised that Paul left the driving seat and came round to open the door and settle her in the passenger seat. She felt a swift surge of liking for him. Any other man would have gone off in a huff at her dismissal, she knew. He was different. He understood that it was the misery of migraine and not pique that made her so brusque, so offhand.

The car rolled gently away from the kerb at a touch. Miranda found herself relaxing for the first time that day. The pain in her head was not now so bad and her stomach seemed to be settling. She wondered whether to thank the sal volatile or the uplift of his caring concern. There were times when it was very pleasant to be looked after, she decided, forgetting how much it had irked her that Edward had wanted to give his life to considering her comfort, her convenience, her every wish.

She reached to touch his hand as it rested on the wheel. 'I am grateful,' she said quietly.

'So you should be after sending me away in that peremptory fashion. I'm an autocrat. That means I don't care to take orders from anyone,' he said drily.

Amused, she said: 'Yes, I know. I'm sorry.'

'Never apologise to me, Miranda.' His tone was suddenly curt. 'It isn't necessary and I don't like it.'

She raised an eyebrow. 'You are a strange man,' she said involuntarily.

'But not a stranger.'

'No, not a stranger,' she agreed slowly. She smiled with sudden warmth. 'I think I've known you all my life.'

'And don't know me at all.'

It was true, of course. She did not know what went on in that handsome dark head. She knew nothing about his way of life except that it was probably disreputable. She did not know his family, his friends, his background. She wanted him and nothing else seemed to matter. But it was very possible that once she knew him better she might not like him at all or approve of him as a person. Their relationship was too superficial, entirely too physical, to last for any length of time, she realised . . . and wondered why she was fool enough to encourage him, to yield to him as she undoubtedly would.

She was silent for a moment, studying his profile against the background of street lighting. It was a very handsome profile and suddenly she melted inside with the warmth of her longing for him. 'Why did you wait?' she asked, curious. 'It seems . . . out of character.'

He glanced at her briefly. In his dark eyes was an expression she had seen before . . . the faint glow that signalled both desire and intent. 'I want you,' he said bluntly, without finesse, without pretence. He was besieged, tormented. She was a fever in his blood and he was used to taking what he wanted when he wanted.

Miranda felt the shock of the words like a

36

blow to the solar plexus. She was a direct person. But he was a little too direct, she felt, startled. She should be chilled, repelled. But her pulses quickened and desire stirred in swift response. 'Oh, entirely in character,' she amended lightly, drily, teasing him. 'You think my resistance at a low ebb!'

He smiled. 'And I've brought an ally.' He jerked his head towards the back of the car. 'Champagne . . .'

'Champagne!' Astonished, she turned and saw the unmistakable bottle in an ice bucket wedged in a corner of the back seat.

'It works wonders for migraine. A glass of ice-cold champagne before I take you to bed and I guarantee that you'll forget your headache in no time at all.'

Miranda did not know whether to laugh or protest. 'You're outrageous!' she exclaimed. Then quite spoiling the effect, she added: 'You must be in league with Polly, my dresser. She declares that marriage cured her of migraine!'

'Well, it wasn't the piece of paper that did the trick,' he said drily. 'I recommend the champagne. It isn't such a drastic remedy.' He turned his head to look at her. 'I don't think I need to say this. But you are aware that I've no intention of marrying you?'

It was the last thing in the world that Miranda wanted. But instinctively she bridled. A woman liked an opportunity to say no, after all. Otherwise she felt as though she had been weighed and found wanting!

'And I've no intention of marrying you,' she returned lightly, brightly. 'I'm glad we've got that out of the way. No false illusions.'

A little smile flickered about his lips. He said gently: 'You see, I am a very good lover—and I enjoy the role. I don't think I could play the husband with any degree of success—or very much enjoyment. Marriage seems to me to be a very dull business.'

As he was only voicing the kind of sentiment that Miranda had expressed herself, to Edward and to others, very many times in the past, it was odd that she felt the instinctive need to disagree with him. Perversity, she told herself firmly . . . sheer perversity . . .

CHAPTER FOUR

It was only a short distance between the theatre and Miranda's flat. The ice about the champagne had not even begun to melt by the time she turned the key in the lock, her heart beating a little too fast, tension tightening her neck muscles and renewing the pain in her temples.

Paul set down the champagne and turned to help her out of her coat. She thanked him with a little smile and he bent his head to touch his lips briefly to the back of her neck. She moved away from him a little too quickly. He smiled, very sure of her response.

Miranda brought glasses. The cork was drawn and the foaming champagne poured and Paul raised his glass in a silent toast before he drank, his dark eyes warm with admiration for her beauty. She was very lovely, quite irresistible. He could not remember when he had last wanted a woman quite so much.

Miranda sat down and leaned her head back against the cushions, briefly closing her eyes against the torment of the light. She wanted him but she wished he would go and leave her in peace.

Paul looked down at her pale face, framed by that beautiful hair. Slowly, deliberately, he bent over her and pressed his lips to the slender throat. He felt the pulse quicken and leap . . . and in a moment she was in his arms.

Miranda caught her breath on a tide of longing. He was without doubt the most exciting man she had ever known, she thought, yielding to the magic of his kiss and discovering with a little shock of surprise that the world really could stand still . . .

Her body was a tingling flame of desire. Nothing mattered but his kiss, his touch, his urgent desire storming to match her own . . . and then the telephone rang, shattering the tension and the tumult.

'Let it ring,' Paul said fiercely against her lips as she made an involuntary movement towards the telephone.

She tried to relax while the bell pealed, insistent. It rang and rang . . . and at last, in sudden desperation, she wrenched herself out of Paul's embrace and snatched up the receiver.

'Miranda . . .?'

It was Edward. Sudden, desperate hunger for her, the need to be with her, the longing to hear her voice at the very least, had driven him to the telephone. Sometimes he was unbearably lonely, aching for her with every fibre of his being.

'Don't you ever give up?' she asked with an impatience that was nevertheless touched with an indulgence that did not escape the listening Paul. He studied her lovely face, watching for the smallest sign that the man's call was more welcome to her than she wished him to know.

'I want to see you,' Edward said without pride.

'When?'

'Now! Tonight! Please, Miranda.'

She was silent. Edward knew with sudden, painful clarity that she was not alone. Anger, jealousy and throbbing anguish struggled for supremacy within him.

'I'm sorry, Edward,' she said at last, harsh because she hated to hurt him. 'But I just don't feel like seeing anyone tonight. I'm in bed with a migraine.'

It was true, she thought wryly. She was in

40

bed and she did have a migraine . . . slight now but persistent. There was absolutely no need to mention Paul who lay beside her and reached for her, running his hands lightly, teasingly, over her slender body even while she talked to Edward. Her words caused him to chuckle softly and she reproached him with a glance that spoke volumes.

Edward sensed rather than heard that choke of laughter in the background . . . and anger overcame all other emotion. 'Warn the poor devil that he won't last any longer than the others,' he said savagely and slammed down the receiver.

He knew there had been other men in the weeks since she had left him. The vibrant sensuality that had given him so much delight would inevitably respond just as readily to another man. He had forced himself to face facts, to accept. But she had deliberately taunted him with an obvious lie, deliberately flaunted a new lover in his face! Without an ounce of sensitivity for his feelings, she had meant him to know that she lay in another man's arms even as she talked on the telephone.

It was so unlike Miranda that it could only mean that he had lost her completely. She no longer cared anything at all for him.

Edward rejected that thought swiftly, stubbornly. She did love him. She had merely lost her way. One day she would realise what she really wanted and come back to him—and he would still be waiting with open arms. Anything else was unthinkable.

He had missed her desperately. Life without Miranda was hell and it did not help that she ran around with a succession of men although well-meaning friends said that the lack of a permanent man in her life was a good sign. It seemed much more likely that in her present state of mind she preferred an unsettled way of life to any kind of life with him!

Yet they had been very happy in the months that they had spent together. He had done all he could to make her happy and it still seemed incredible that she could just stop loving without cause. He refused to believe that she had never really loved him at all.

Her insistence on freedom was the root cause of it all, of course. But they were right for each other and he knew that she loved him and one day she would accept that marriage was not the prison she feared but a commitment that was welcomed by two people who truly loved each other. She would come back to him and they would be happy again.

That belief had sustained him for weeks. Loving Miranda, he refused to despair—and he had also refused to look for consolation in the arms of other women. Now, angry, hurt, humiliated by the woman he loved, he wondered if he was the fool that his friends declared him to be. Perhaps he had gone the wrong way to bring Miranda back to him. Tamely waiting around, refusing to look at another woman, declaring that he still loved and wanted her had not brought results. Perhaps he should have shown her that she was not the only woman in the world, after all!

He had all the bright memories of the past. He had all the determined hope for the future. But the present was a lonely time for him and suddenly, quite unbidden, he remembered the warm friendliness of the young nurse he had met at a party. He had dismissed Julia as a nice girl but not to be compared with the lovely, exciting, wholly desirable Miranda. Now he recalled her with sudden clarity and wondered if he had been too hasty . . .

He would never have gone to that party if Miranda had kept her promise to meet him. Waiting in the crowded bar long after the appointed time, finally accepting that she did not mean to come, Edward had suddenly become angry, suddenly despised his own weakness in wanting a woman who no longer wanted him, suddenly remembered that Clare Cloud had invited him to her party . . . and on impulse he had gone to it, arriving late but finding a warm welcome. There he had met Julia and liked her and known instinctively that she liked him . . .

Miranda replaced the receiver, feeling slightly sick. When she remembered how dear he had been and all that they had been to each other, she despised herself for lying to Edward, for hurting him.

Paul slid his arms about her, drawing her close. She resisted instinctively. His eyes narrowed abruptly. Another man might have released her, sensitive to her reluctance. His arms tightened, forcing her slender body against his own. He kissed her, demanding rather than seeking response. But her heart was not in it, he knew . . . and he was abruptly, savagely angry.

'Damn you!' he said, releasing her, even thrusting her away. 'No woman lies in my arms and thinks about another man!'

'Damn you!' she retorted with spirit, her sapphire eyes sparkling. 'I do as I please!'

'If it pleases you to think about Kane while I make love to you then I'm losing my touch,' he said with wry humour.

Temper subsided. She looked at him and laughed softly. He was so unpredictable. One never knew what he would do or say—and she liked that! She leaned towards him, kissed him slowly, tantalisingly, making amends. His lips were cold, unresponsive. It seemed that all desire had left him. She looked into dark eyes that seemed to be scarcely aware of her and felt a hint of panic. She did not want to lose him because Edward could not let her go!

She rested her cheek on his powerful chest, felt the heavy beat of his heart. 'If I wanted Edward I would be with him,' she said quietly.

He twined his fingers in her thick, gleaming hair. 'Bury your dead, Miranda. I always do.'

She was still, disliking the thought of the women he had known and discarded and apparently forgotten with such ease. How long before she joined the list, she wondered bleakly.

'I'm fond of Edward,' she said slowly, a little stubbornly. 'And I like to keep my friends.'

He moved impatiently. 'Sentimental and stupid! And damnably unfair to any man. Let him go, Miranda!' He was thankful that he had never allowed his heart to rule his head. He had seen the misery that could come of loving. Numerous disappointed women had accused him of having no heart. Paul had never disputed the matter. Women stirred him physically and bored him quickly and he would not subscribe to the nonsense of self-deception that was commonly called love.

Miranda hesitated. Then her chin tilted almost defiantly. No man had ever told her how to run her life! 'But I might want him again one day.'

'An honest woman!' he exclaimed, amused. 'There we have the crux of the matter. You might want him again one day—and it suits you to keep him dangling on a string in the meantime. A typical woman's trick!'

She lifted a slender shoulder. 'He loves me.' Inevitably this affair would end and although she had no intention of falling in love with

Paul Keller, it might hurt a little to lose him—and she might be glad to turn to someone like Edward for comfort. But she did not expect Paul to understand a woman's need for that kind of insurance, she thought wryly.

'Poor fool! I've yet to discover what it is about you that keeps him on that string,' he drawled. 'You're beautiful, amusing, exciting—but just a woman like all the others I've known. Easily replaced and easily forgotten.'

'Devil . . .!' she exclaimed, laughing, pummelling him with her fists.

He caught her hands and held them firmly, looked directly into her smiling eyes. 'You think I am not serious? I am! You imagine you are something special in my life? You're not! Tonight I want you, but tomorrow someone else might come along and you will be unimportant. That's the way I live, the way I like it. No ties.'

Strangely, her heart sank. Strangely, because he echoed her own thoughts and feelings of the past. Why should she feel differently where he was concerned? He was a man like any other. A little more exciting than most but just a man! She could replace him with the merest lift of a finger!

She felt an odd pang, a hollowness in the pit of her stomach, a little clutch of fear at his words. But she would have died rather than let him know it. They were two of a kind, she told herself firmly. Take the here and now and let tomorrow take care of itself!

She put her arms about him on a swift surge of wanting. 'Tonight is all that matters . . .' she whispered . . . and kissed him.

Miranda woke in the morning, still marvelling. She had not known that mere mortals could be given a glimpse of heaven! She had not known that a mere man could transport her to paradise with his embrace. Smiling at the contentment that still welled within her, she turned her head to look at Paul, sleeping like a child. She put out a hand to touch him as though she doubted the reality of his presence. Instantly he was awake, aware of her—and, it seemed to Miranda, rejecting any suggestion that the shared delights of the night were of any real importance. He kissed her briefly, carelessly, and rolled over to read his watch.

Within a very short time, he was gone . . . and Miranda wandered aimlessly about the flat, missing him to a ridiculous extent and wondering what it was about him that she liked so much. He was graceless and arrogant, entirely selfish, taking what he wanted and to hell with the consequences. He seemed to have little or no respect for women. He lived by his own rules. He was the kind of man she had always disliked and despised. But she was utterly incapable of refusing to see him again—and she was terrified that he would tire of her long before she tired of him!

He came back to take her to lunch and she learned that he had spent most of the morning rearranging a very busy schedule so that they could be together as much as possible for the next few days. Miranda was surprised and delighted but she took him to task for assuming that she had nothing better to do with her leisure hours than spend them with him.

He laughed. 'If you have better things to do then go ahead, Miranda. I'm not tying you down to anything. But I think you'll want to be with me.'

'You're damnably sure of yourself,' she said slowly, a little tartly.

'Sure of you,' he amended, smiling. He took her hand and carried it to his lips. 'Silly girl! Make the most of me while you can. I'm as fickle as you are!'

She was conscious of interested eyes and wished he had not brought her to the *Caprice*, that most famous of restaurants frequented by the famous, mostly from the world of show business. She did not doubt that Paul Keller was known to most of the gossips, as much for his doubtful reputation as a link in London's underworld as for his position in London's society as owner of very successful nightclubs and casinos. She might not be so easily recognised, she thought modestly, but there must be some who could put a name to her face and link it with Paul for the benefit of

48

every interested party in town. She could almost hear the murmur of comment that circulated about the room. For Paul was very open in his admiration, his attentiveness. It was flattering but a little disconcerting when she was not sure how much of it was genuine.

'Your play is coming off at the end of another week,' he said, surprising her with his knowledge of something she had not even suspected. 'It's losing a great deal of money. Kovak wanted to close down this week but he's been talked into giving it another chance. You've nothing else lined up. I thought we might go down to Cornwall. I have a house by the sea and I'm overdue for a holiday.'

Miranda agreed without betraying eagerness. She fancied that he was the kind of man to draw back at the very first indication that he was becoming more important to a woman than he could wish.

He was very casual, very light-hearted about their relationship and she felt it would be wise to follow his lead. At the moment, it looked as though their affair might last longer than she had expected or dared to hope. Perhaps he liked her more than those other women who had briefly enjoyed his attentions. She decided not to question anything but just to go along with anything he wanted and see where the path led.

There was no need to have everything cut and dried in life, after all. Sometimes it was more exciting not to know what the future held. Sometimes it was relaxing just to drift, to play it by ear. Edward had always wanted to make plans for the future and she had never been sure that they had a future at all. She disliked making plans and she always tried not to look forward to anything too much, having learned that disappointment was always waiting around the corner for the unwary optimist.

She was determined not to dwell on the prospect of those few days in Cornwall, alone with him, away from everyone and everything else. But her heart leaped so much at the very thought that she was forced to remind herself sternly that she had no intention of making a fool of herself by falling in love with a man like Paul Keller . . .

CHAPTER FIVE

Miranda was on her way to meet Paul. Paying off her taxi in Shaftesbury Avenue, she suddenly saw a familiar figure and her heart contracted unexpectedly. Tall and very blond, Edward was striding purposefully through the crowd.

'Edward . . . !'

He turned towards her swiftly, eagerly. She smiled at him across the pavement . . . a smile of such breathtaking sweetness and warmth that he caught his breath and took a step towards her, his heart leaping with all the optimism of a lover. So had she smiled in the early days of their relationship.

It was some time since they had met. Edward tried to remember just how long and was astonished that it was not engraved on his heart. Missing her as he did, it seemed impossible that he was not aware of the exact amount of days since he had seen her. Ten, eleven . . . he could not be sure. Life, even without Miranda, was lived at such a pace that days merged into each other.

He reached her and she looked up at him, smiling. 'Edward . . .' she said again, giving him both her hands. It was impulsive, possibly foolish. But she warmed to him as she saw the eager look in his very blue eyes. Dear Edward. He still cared, she thought with swift concern. She was so happy in her relationship with Paul that it grieved her to think of all the unhappiness that she had caused by not loving Edward as he loved her.

He took her hands, gripped them tightly . . . hands that had held him, caressed him. Hands that he loved for their slender beauty. 'Darling,' he said softly, tenderly, love for her flooding him in that moment. Nothing had changed. Nothing could ever change the way he felt about her.

'Nice to see you,' she said gently.

51

He drew her hand through his arm possessively. 'Come and have a drink.'

'Ten minutes,' she warned. 'I'm meeting a friend. I'm early or I wouldn't have run into you.' She squeezed his arm. 'I'm glad I did.'

He guided her through the press of people, almost overwhelmed with emotion. She had that effect on him, stunning him with her beauty, filling him with instant desire. For the first time in days, she had been far from his thoughts. Seeing her was a considerable jolt to his emotions.

Miranda could not help being pleased, a little flattered, by the warmth of his delight at their encounter. She did not want him to be unhappy but it was heartwarming and flattering and very reassuring to realise how much power she had to sway a man's emotions. One smile and Edward was her slave, she thought wryly . . . and wished she could say the same for Paul!

Edward was a dear. She was really very fond of him. He knew just how to make a woman feel like a queen, a goddess . . . Paul only knew how to make a woman feel like a woman! Sometimes she missed Edward very much. There was no one quite like him, after all . . . and it seemed that he still felt there was no one quite like her.

They found a quiet corner in a pub and he bought drinks. He looked at her with a little smile in his eyes as he sat down. 'I'm very angry with you,' he said, his tone belying the words. 'You stood me up the other night.'

'I know,' she said lightly, unrepentant. 'Suddenly it just didn't seem a good idea to meet you. I hope you didn't wait too long for me.'

'No. I went to a party instead,' he said coolly.

She smiled. 'I'm glad. Any nice girls?'

'One in particular,' he agreed. A man had his pride, after all—and Julia *was* a nice girl. Much too good for him . . .

'Good.' She was untroubled. She smiled again and said frankly: 'You were right, you know. I did have someone with me when you rang.'

A nerve jumped in his jaw. 'You don't have to explain anything to me,' he said brusquely, preferring not to think of her in another man's arms. 'You're a free agent. That's what you wanted, wasn't it?'

'Oh, I'm not explaining. I don't regret a thing—except hurting you,' she said with truth. 'It wasn't that I didn't want to see you, Edward. I always like to see you. It's just . . . well, it wasn't convenient.'

He nodded. There was pain in his eyes and in the set of his mouth. 'I'm as jealous as hell,' he said grimly. 'And there's nothing I can do about it.'

'You could try loving me less,' she said quietly.

He smiled wryly. 'I seem to be a one-woman man.'

'Then I can't help you.'

'You could marry me. Isn't that supposed to be a cure for love?'

She sighed. 'Please, Edward.'

'Sorry! I didn't mean to propose. I know how you feel about marriage,' he said bitterly.

'I wish you understood,' she said sharply.

'Well, I don't. I love you. I want to marry you and look after you—and you behave as though I'm insulting you.'

'Let's talk about something else,' she said firmly. 'You're still at the *National*?'

'For a few more days. Your play comes off at the end of the week, doesn't it?' He reached for her hand. 'We both need a holiday. Come away with me, Miranda. We'll go to Greece and I'll persuade you to love me all over again. And I won't mention marriage once—I swear it!'

'No, Edward,' she said, laughing. 'I'm going to Cornwall with a friend . . . it's all arranged.'

He tossed off his drink. 'A man?'

'A man,' she agreed coolly. She had never lied to him. 'Paul Keller.'

He swore. 'He won't bore you with talk of marriage, anyway,' he said drily. 'Like you, he reacts as though it's the plague by all accounts.' He had been shocked by the rumour that she had become the mistress of a notorious rake and near-criminal and he had refused to believe it. But she had not only admitted it. She almost seemed proud of the fact, he thought bitterly.

'And that suits me very well,' Miranda said. 'No strings attached. We can enjoy each other without guilt.' Unconsciously she quoted Paul's words.

Edward had always admired her honesty but there were times when it could be brutal. 'Send me a card,' he said wearily, defeated, despairing.

'But you'll be in Greece.'

'Not without you.'

She reproached him with the smile in her eyes. 'Don't be silly, darling. There must be a dozen girls who'd leap at the chance of a holiday with you.'

'You flatter me.'

'I mean it. You're a very attractive man, Edward. Heavens, you don't need me to tell you so! There were plenty of girls before me! Don't be a spoiled brat . . . denied a particular sweet and declaring all the others taste nasty when you won't even try one!' She laughed softly, teasing him.

Sudden anger swept him that she cared so little when he had given so much. 'I might just take your advice,' he said without warmth.

She picked up her bag. 'I'm late. I'll ring you when I get back to town and we'll have lunch or dinner or something.' She laid cool fingers on his cheek. 'Don't care so much,' she said with sudden vehemence. 'You'll be a lot happier. Find a nice girl who wants a husband, home, kids. Forget me, Edward. Because I won't come back to you. I'll never marry you.'

'Oh, Miranda . . .' he said, achingly.

Her fingers moved swiftly to still his lips. 'Don't make me sorry that we met,' she warned. 'Be sensible and we can go on being friends. But I won't be proposed to every time we meet!'

He smiled wryly. 'I'm a bore.'

'Yes, you are. I know you love me. I love you too—in my own way. But I must be free and I've told you that a thousand times.'

'Come home and I'll never mention marriage again,' he vowed. 'We'll be together and that's all I care about.'

She shook her head. 'That's a promise you can't keep,' she said carefully, knowing him very well. 'I know it and so do you. Marriage matters to you, Edward. All right. That's the kind of man you are and I accept it. Please accept the kind of person I am. I'm not interested in getting married . . . not now, not ever!'

'And particularly not to me,' he said bitterly.

She would not be drawn. She took up her bag and rose to her feet. 'I wish you'd find someone else, Edward,' she said gently. She kissed him lightly on the top of his blond head and left him.

Edward looked after her, tense, angry,

knowing the familiar sense of frustration. His heart hammered at the very thought of her with Paul Keller. Damn her! It would serve her right if he took her bloody stupid advice! Julia was a pretty little plum just ripe for the picking—and she would marry him tomorrow if he wished it! It was not a conceit. Julia, warm and generous and very sweet, made no effort to conceal the way she felt about him . . . and he did not deny that it comforted a man to know that someone cared for him. He loved Miranda dearly but she was entirely without heart. How could she take up with a rogue and a rake like Keller and flaunt the affair so openly? How much had changed in a very short time from the girl who had loved him, lived with him, given him so much happiness . . .

Miranda was late and it worried her. For it was not wise to keep Paul waiting, she had found. It would be surprising if he had waited, she thought wryly. She was reluctant to annoy him just when the trip to Cornwall seemed to be reality rather than a vague suggestion. He might cancel it at a moment's notice—or replace her with any of a dozen women. It ought not to matter but it did. She would be flooded with disappointment if she did not have those few days with him, away from all distractions. He was sensual, selfish, a little cruel, utterly unpredictable—but he possessed a fatal fascination for her and she could not stop thinking about him, wanting him, longing

57

to be with him.

He was a very different man to Edward. Paul was as honest and direct as herself, making no pretence that loving had anything to do with their fierce passion for each other, making no promise that their future lay with each other. She was entirely free to continue their relationship or to end it as she pleased . . . and so was he. He made no demands on her that she could not meet.

Edward was a dear and she did love him— how could she help it? But he wanted to own her, body and soul. Miranda found it stifling and she was thankful for the kind of careless, casual, undemanding excitement that she found with Paul.

He was at the bar, talking idly to one of the barmen. He did not look at her as she entered and crossed to the stool by his side . . . not even following her progress as it was reflected in the long bar mirror. He seemed utterly unaware of her. But he looked at his wristwatch, slim and gold and very expensive.

Miranda smiled and slid an arm about his neck, kissed him lightly. 'Sorry . . . I was held up by the traffic.'

He removed her arm from his neck and his fingers were vice-like on her slender wrist. 'You were with Kane in the *Fountain*,' he corrected smoothly.

She bit her lip. 'Yes.' She should have known that she could not hide anything from him. He had friends and contacts all over Soho and little seemed to escape him if he made it his business to know what was going on in a certain quarter.

'Why not say so?' he drawled. His dark eyes rested on her face without warmth or welcome.

He was right, of course. There was no reason to conceal the fact that she had met Edward. She was free to meet her friends whenever she wished. She did not have to answer to Paul who had no jealousy of Edward or anyone else. He did not care enough to be jealous.

'I ran into Edward in Shaftesbury Avenue and we had a drink together,' she said lightly.

'I don't object to that. But don't lie to me.' He released her wrist. The indentations of his fingers on the soft flesh hinted at bruising to come. He followed her rueful glance. Then, smiling his slow, sensual smile, he raised her hand and touched his lips to the marks of his fingers . . . and a little shiver rippled through her body. He heard the swift catch of her breath and knew that she was still in thrall to him. 'You're beautiful,' he said quietly. 'But I won't share you, Miranda.'

'Edward and I . . . it's over, completely. I've told you,' she said firmly.

He nodded. 'Keep it that way. Or say goodbye to me.'

It was a command. He was very autocratic

and Miranda marvelled that she submitted so meekly when she had always cherished her independence. He was very spoiled, of course. No one had ever said nay to him, it seemed, least of all women—and she knew that she was as weak as all the others before her. It was something about him that held her almost against her will and it was not just his expertise as a lover that carried her to heights of ecstacy she had not known to exist.

Over lunch, he talked at length of Cornwall for the first time, describing the remote village and his house on the cliff-top overlooking the sea. It was his escape from the grime and glitter of his life in London and he spoke of Penmawr with a warmth that surprised Miranda who saw him as so right against the Soho setting that it was difficult to visualise him against any other background. She was looking forward so much to the holiday . . . some days with him away from all other distractions and considerations. He was an amusing, interesting companion as well as an exciting lover, she had discovered.

She said warmly: 'It's going to be fun, Paul . . . just you and me and to hell with the rest of the world!' She laid her hand on his arm, smiling into his eyes.

Paul drank a little wine. It had always been his intention to take her to Cornwall and leave the rest of the world behind for a few days. But he did not like to be taken for granted . . . and he particularly disliked that possessive hand on his arm, that glowing confidence in her sapphire eyes. It seemed that she was no different to any other woman, after all. A few days of his undivided attention and she began to think she owned him!

He said carelessly: 'It's a party, my dear . . . twelve or fourteen people. I owe hospitality to several friends and I like to have lots of people about me.' He saw the flicker of disappointment in her eyes and he laughed softly. 'You're a great girl, Miranda. But there's more to life than making love. We'd bore each other in three days if we didn't have other company, other conversation.'

Miranda had not known quite how much she wanted those days with him, away from everyone and everything that had a claim on his time and attention. She had not known quite how intensely she felt about him—and it was a shock. For she was not a jealous or possessive person. She knew he was right. She agreed with him . . . with her level head. But it seemed that instinct was a very different matter!

'It's your party,' she said carelessly. But she was filled with sudden angry frustration and it betrayed itself in the fierce clenching of her fingers on the slender stem of her wine-glass. Unexpectedly, it snapped.

The wine stained the pristine cloth. A waiter was immediately on hand to remove the broken glass and cope with the staining liquid. A fresh glass was provided and more wine poured . . . and Paul sat silent, a brooding amusement in his dark eyes, knowing exactly the tensions that had caused the accident to happen.

A glass splinter had cut her hand . . . only slightly but enough to draw blood. She dabbed at it with a handkerchief, angry and embarrassed and doing her best to appear cool and unconcerned. Paul reached for a sliver of glass that had escaped the waiter's notice. Deliberately, with Miranda's startled gaze on him, he punctured the top of a finger. Then, smiling and with an expression she could not analyse in his eyes, he took her hand and mingled their blood. He leaned across the table to kiss her on the mouth with sudden urgency.

'You're mine for as long as I want you,' he said softly, against her lips. 'Don't forget it.'

Miranda felt the shock of the action about her heart. It was such an odd and surprising thing for him to do, she felt. He was not a man who readily committed himself to anyone or anything. Yet there had been commitment in the way he deliberately cut his own hand so that their blood should flow together. Wasn't that the way gipsies celebrated a wedding? American Indians? Or was it a Jewish ritual? Did Paul Keller, rake and rogue who was reputed to care for nobody but himself, care enough to claim her as his own in that strange fashion? And did she want to belong to him?

Miranda was suddenly not at all sure what she did want . . .

CHAPTER SIX

Edward was relaxed, enjoying himself, content in the company of people he liked. And it was a lively luncheon party at the *Caprice* with Clare Cloud, who had been such a successful Rosalind to his Orlando in *As You Like It*, and her cousins Allister and Julia. Like almost every Cloud, Allister was an actor. The Clouds were a famous theatrical family, much-loved. But Julia had chosen to nurse.

Edward had become very fond of Julia in a very short time and he knew that she loved him. She was very warm and generous in her loving and in all fairness he ought to break with her before she became too involved, he thought wryly. He had too little to give—and she was giving too much. He knew what it meant to love deeply and he did not want Julia to suffer as he suffered. In all fairness, he ought to end the relationship which had drifted so naturally into an affair. But he felt an odd wrench of reluctance to part with her. Just now, he needed someone like Julia who gave without demanding anything in return.

Just now, he needed the loving and the laughter that he found in her arms. Her sweetness soothed the tumult of heart and mind. Her warm embrace comforted his loneliness. It might be wrong and selfish to cling to her but he could not give her up . . . not yet!

She was happy and it pleased him to see the radiance in her small, pretty face. It would take a more ruthless man than himself to erase the glowing happiness from those candid grey eyes . . . and he could not help feeling that he would be very much the loser.

Miranda was never going to come back to him. He was accepting that truth at last. It was almost a relief to be free of the hoping and the need that had tormented him during all the weeks since she had walked out of his life. He loved her still, would always love her. But he was beginning to discover that the world had not ended with her failure to love him, after all. Julia loved him and perhaps he could find a measure of happiness with Julia . . .

Conversation and laughter flowed as readily as the wine and Edward was relaxed, enjoying the occasion which had somehow turned into a party with the chance meeting with Julia's brother and a friend.

Suddenly, he knew an odd little prickle of awareness at the back of his neck. He swivelled in his chair, knowing instinctively that Miranda had walked into the restaurant . . . and there she was, on Keller's arm, head high as though she defied him to resent her intimacy with the man. The whole town seemed to be talking about their affair but she apparently did not mind that her name was linked with the man who had such a doubtful reputation, not only where women were concerned.

Instinctively, Edward half-rose from his seat. He wanted to go to her, to claim her, to whisk her from that crowded restaurant and take her home. She was so beautiful and he loved her so much, missed her so terribly. In the small house where once they had been so happy, they could be happy again if only she would give him a chance to prove it. She could not be as indifferent as she pretended if her gaze could find him so swiftly in a crowd where she could not even have expected him to be— and Edward was sure that her heart had contracted like his own when their eyes met across the room . . .

Miranda checked involuntarily at the sight of Edward. Her hand tightened on Paul's arm. It must seem like a betrayal, she realised, as he stiffened slightly. But she was filled with alarm rather than delight, dreading a confrontation between the two men. Paul was not a jealous man and he had no need to be jealous of Edward. But Edward was sufficiently moved by love for her to create a scene even in a gossip-ridden haunt like the *Caprice*—and Paul would hate it although he would only brush it aside with contempt.

For once she was not warmed or flattered by the intense emotion in the blue eyes that held her own across the room. To be loved so much was a responsibility, she realised with an unexpected qualm. She was very, very fond of Edward. But if he said or did anything to threaten the delicate balance of her relationship with Paul, she might not find it easy to forgive him!

People were staring, whispering . . . and it was infuriating that they must stand and wait for an eternity while a table was organised for them. Paul was unusually patient, a little smile hovering about that sensual mouth . . . and she fancied that he was enjoying her discomfiture.

Her affair with Edward and the manner of its ending must be common knowledge to their own kind who frequented the *Caprice* . . . and no doubt everyone waited for Edward to challenge the man who had taken his place in her life. Miranda devoutly hoped that he would not give them that kind of satisfaction. Why on earth had Paul insisted on bringing her to this particular restaurant today of all days? With thankfulness she saw that a table had been found and she decided to smile, waggle her fingers in careless greeting, for to snub Edward would only give the gossips even more to talk about.

Paul had other ideas. His dark eyes had narrowed and they missed nothing. He was aware of Miranda's dismay if not its exact cause, of Kane's passionate and primitive desire to fell him with one blow and carry Miranda off to the love-nest they had once shared, of Julia Cloud's stricken face that told its own story and the keen interest that the erstwhile lovers were attracting on all sides.

He said smoothly: 'One can always be sure of running into friends in this place . . . and it's a mistake to risk offending them. Come and meet the Clouds . . . or do you know them already? It's a small world, after all.' And, inexorably, a firm hand at her elbow, he guided her across the room towards the table where Edward sat with his companions—and there was an amused challenge in the dark eyes.

Miranda was an actress. So she walked by Paul's side as though she welcomed an introduction to his friends and had absolutely no reason to shrink from a meeting with the man who had so recently been her lover.

Edward's hands clenched. There was insolence in Keller's attitude and his easy familiarity towards Miranda was intolerable, deliberately emphasised, he felt. He seethed—and his anger was surprisingly directed more at Miranda who had given Keller the right to parade her in public as his latest love. No one in the *Caprice*, watching with such interest, could doubt the degree of intimacy between them, he thought bitterly—or be in ignorance of the fact that Miranda had left him to walk into Keller's arms within a very short time.

Allister Cloud eased the first moments by welcoming Paul with friendly warmth. They had known each other for years, not intimately but well enough, and he made it appear to any interested observer close enough to overhear that Paul and Miranda had come for the express purpose of greeting him. He was very conscious of his sister's pallour, the dismay that had chased the happiness from her grey eyes, the fear that Miranda Lynch still threatened her love for Edward Kane that had obviously caught at her heart. He was concerned and anxious to protect her as much as possible.

Paul shook hands and responded easily. He nodded to Allister's friend, a slight acquaintance. He smiled down at Julia, a surprisingly warm smile.

'Julia . . .' he said gently with just a hint of kindliness that few people had found in him. He stopped to kiss her soft cheek, claiming the privilege of long acquaintance. He had always liked Julia Cloud, considering her to be the nicest of a very attractive and personable family. He knew all about her feeling for Edward Kane and wished her well and thought she could do very much better for herself. Kane had charm and he was a very successful actor and he never lacked for friends. But if he meant to go on loving Miranda, then he was a fool . . .

Julia smiled at him doubtfully. She had never been quite sure about Paul Keller. There were too many rumours about him and his way of life that were disturbing. She disliked the warmth in his eyes and voice, wondering at it, hoping that no one would misconstrue the look in his dark eyes, the hint of intimacy in the way he rested his hand on her shoulder. Everyone knew that he was a rake with dozens of affairs to his credit. He did not kiss her cousin Clare, she noticed, although they had known each other just as long. She suspected that he had kissed her only to annoy Edward. Yet how could he possibly know that she and Edward were friends . . . rather more than friends now, she reminded herself, not regretting for a moment that she had given with love when he needed her. She only regretted that he was still unable to forget his love for the beautiful, heartless Miranda Lynch . . .

Miranda responded with her easy charm to introductions. Julia's coolness was scarcely noticed and perfectly understood for Miranda was used to instinctive hostility from her own sex. She had not attached much importance to the rumours that linked Edward with the girl.

'You two know each other, of course,' Allister said with only a hint of hesitation, coming to Edward.

'Indeed we do,' she said warmly, easily,

smiling as though there was not the least embarrassment in a meeting between them. Why should there be?

'Intimately,' he agreed smoothly, angry, the smile that touched his lips failing to reach his blue eyes.

Miranda was surprised. For there was a hint of contempt, of anger, even of ice in his expression. She was dismayed. Even when they had quarrelled, the passion had been all on her side. Edward had always been patient, tolerant, quiet of voice and gentle of manner, warm and loving. Making it impossible to go on being angry and even more impossible to leave him—until the day when she had known she must make the break before he whittled away all her instinctive resistance to marriage.

He was abruptly an Edward she did not recognise, hard and cold, looking at her almost with dislike. Perhaps he had ceased to love her, after all. Perhaps she had been supplanted by the pale and silent girl beside him who was so carefully not looking at him or anyone else. Well, it was just what she had wanted so why should she feel an odd little clutch of dismay about her heart?

Paul's mouth tightened at the deliberate provocation of that one word. Jealousy was something he had never experienced in his life until that moment. But suddenly he knew a fierce and jealous resentment of the intimacy that had once existed between the actor and

70

Miranda. He smiled mockingly. 'We must get together and compare notes, Kane,' he said smoothly. 'I like to profit from the mistakes of my predecessors in these matters—and I imagine that you made several.'

There was a shocked silence while everyone wondered if he had actually spoken the words and the blood rushed into Miranda's lovely face. Then Edward was on his feet, anger blazing at the public insult to the woman he loved. 'Bloody swine . . .' He swung a blow that should have connected fair and square with the man's jaw. But Paul was ready for him, parried the blow with his right and followed through with a left to Edward's chin that sent him crashing against the table with its array of plates and glasses and instantly all was confusion and chaos.

The *maitre d'* had been hovering, expecting trouble. Now he rushed forward, voluble in his dismay and indignation, ready to blame everyone but the man who was known and feared because of his influential contacts with the underworld.

'Send me the bill for the damage,' Paul said carelessly. Then, taking the shocked Miranda firmly by the arm, he swept her from the restaurant.

She was shaking as she sat in the car by his side. Once she had foolishly imagined that it would be exciting to have two men fighting over her. Now she knew it was a horrid

71

experience—and she was sick with the fear that Edward had been badly hurt. Yet she had allowed Paul to hustle her away while others fussed about Edward, slumped on the floor and quite unconscious, a trickle of blood at the corner of his mouth.

She despised her weakness for a man who did not hesitate to humiliate her. She was angry, with herself and with him. At the same time, she was afraid of losing him even while she wondered what it was about him that held her so firmly.

'You needn't have hit him so hard,' she said with reproach.

He glanced at her with dry amusement. 'It would have been noble to allow him to hit me, of course. You would have preferred it, I daresay.'

'Yes,' she said, low-voiced, knowing he could not be expected to understand her feeling that Edward was entitled to some satisfaction.

'He isn't your husband. He wasn't even your lover when we met. I've done the man no injury. So why the hell should I take anything he cares to hand out?' he demanded impatiently.

'It might have made him feel better.'

He laughed grimly. 'It wouldn't have done me much good.' She was silent. He turned and pulled her to him with rough hands, kissed her with an urgency that repelled rather than attracted, and felt her shrink from the touch of his lips, the contact with his body. 'Kiss me, damn you!' he said violently. 'Or get the hell out of it and go back to Kane! I won't have half-measures!'

Miranda knew she should push him away, get out of the car and walk away with the determination never to see or speak to him again. Paul Keller was not and never would be any good for her. He was selfish and cruel and ruthless, concerned only with his own desires. He took what he wanted and he did not give a damn for anyone who stood in his way. He was the kind of man she most disliked. So how had she ever become entangled with him? And why did she panic at the mere thought of never seeing him again? And why was she suddenly very sure that her lack of response had caused him pain and forced those angry words from him?

'Paul, I believe you're jealous,' she said slowly, astonished, a little dismayed.

'I told you, Miranda. You're mine while I want you,' he returned savagely.

She knew she should resent his arrogance. Strangely the passion behind his words touched and warmed the heart that seemed unable to decide what it wanted most . . . the emotional security of the kind of loving that Edward offered or the turbulent seas of emotion with a demanding, difficult and even dangerous man such as Paul.

'And when you no longer want me . . .? There was just a touch of apprehension behind the words.

He shrugged. 'When it happens, worry.'

'Edward is a much better bet than you are,' she said slowly.

'Then go back to him.' He was cold, utterly indifferent.

But Miranda caught just a glimpse of anger in the dark eyes and her heart lifted. She smiled at him suddenly. 'Perhaps I will,' she said, provocative. 'But not just yet . . .' She leaned to touch her lips to the sensual, slightly cruel mouth.

Instantly his arms enfolded her in an embrace that held something of tenderness as well as quick-fired passion. 'You are a bitch,' he said softly, his tone transforming the harsh epithet into an endearment. 'But a beautiful bitch . . .' He kissed her with sudden urgency, almost savagely.

She made no secret of his attraction for her, he thought with wryness. She might still care for Kane but she obviously found an excitement in his arms that the actor could not provide. Sentiment apparently held her to Kane. But the fierce sensuality of her nature found greater satisfaction in their affair. Well, he did not ask for more from any woman, he reminded himself.

Yet he found himself disliking the thought that she was keeping Kane in reserve until she tired of him. He did not care for the thought that she was matching him at his own game. It was all very well for a man to enjoy casual affairs wherever and whenever the fancy took him. But he discovered an oddly old-fashioned dislike of it in a woman . . . and particularly Miranda . . .

At the touch of his lips everything, even Edward, was instantly forgotten. She was breathless, caught up in the whirlwind of desire that he aroused so swiftly. Wanting him, she was utterly thankful that he still wanted her. She had been so afraid that the scene in the restaurant would have dire repercussions.

Consumed with a longing that was not entirely physical, she stroked his dark hair and revelled in the strength of his arms about her. Nothing in the world seemed to matter in that moment but their continued need of each other.

'Take me home, Paul . . .' she whispered huskily, with warm invitation.

He released her and set the car in motion at her bidding. But he was unusually silent as they drove through the lunch-time traffic.

Miranda did not notice. She was much too eager to melt into his arms once more, to know again that rush of emotion that might or might not be loving but was stronger than anything she had ever experienced in the past . . .

CHAPTER SEVEN

Paul abruptly made up his mind.

Bringing the car to a halt outside the block of apartments, he made no move to get out but leaned across to open the passenger door with a casualness that was almost offensive. 'I'll ring you,' he said carelessly.

Miranda's heart plunged with disappointment, with disbelief. 'But . . . aren't you coming in?'

'I've things to do.' He was almost curt. He did not expect her to understand his sudden revulsion of feeling. He did not understand it himself.

Her heart swelled at the indifference of his tone. 'Don't play games with me, Paul,' she said, abruptly angry.

He touched her flushed cheek with the back of his fingers in a light, meaningless caress. 'I'll ring you,' he repeated, refusing to relent. He needed time to think, to sort out emotions that threatened to turn his life upside down.

Anger soared. 'When the mood takes you?' Her chin tilted. 'Well, you may not find me at home!'

He raised an amused eyebrow. 'Then I shall know where to find you, won't I?' he said drily. 'But don't expect me to come looking.'

Her hands clenched in her lap. She was

terrified of saying or doing the wrong thing, of alienating him completely. She was puzzled by the abrupt change of his mood. And she was frightened by the implication that this was suddenly the end of their affair. How did one hold a man like Paul, she wondered in sudden desperation. He despised weakness, distrusted sentiment, drew back from the slightest hint of possessiveness.

Miranda struggled with the blazing temper that had cost her too many things she dearly wanted in the past. She must keep her cool. She must not walk away from this man in anger or she would certainly never see him again—and the very thought was unbearable, stabbing her with sudden pain. She was alarmed. Had he become so important, so necessary to her happiness?

'You can't expect me to sit around waiting for you to call like . . . like a neglected wife,' she said lightly, very carefully. 'I'm not used to such cavalier treatment, Paul. I don't like it.'

'Few women do,' he said drily.

She knew a surge of resentment at the reminder of all the other women he had known and lightly loved. 'You're so cold-blooded,' she said angrily. 'Why do you hold back, refuse to commit yourself, insist that you don't give a damn for anyone! You just can't give yourself, can you? Not to me . . . not to any woman!'

He turned his head to look at her and there

was a coldness she had never seen in his dark, glittering eyes. Her heart sank with dismay.

'When you start to give, maybe I will,' he said quietly but with telling force. 'When you can commit yourself wholeheartedly to a man then perhaps I'll be capable of loving. And you're talking about loving, aren't you, Miranda? You must be loved . . . by Kane, by me! Nothing else will satisfy you. Well, when I am convinced that you can care for someone other than yourself then I might begin to care for you!'

Miranda was shocked. She looked down at her hands, feeling as though he had struck her. Was that really how she seemed to him . . . shallow, selfish, superficial? She supposed it was true. She took but she did not want to give too much. She liked to be loved but did not wish to love in return. She was reluctant to commit herself to a lasting affair. But why should that concern Paul? It suited him very well, after all. He was as shallow, as selfish, as superficial as herself!

'I care about people!' she protested with some heat. 'You certainly don't! Sometimes I think you like to hurt. Today . . . at the *Caprice*! You wanted to hurt Edward, didn't you? You enjoyed goading him—and you liked it even more when you could hit him with justification. That was . . . primitive!'

'Yes,' he agreed, remembering the flood of jealous anger and the satisfaction it had given him to knock the man to the floor. 'That's just what it was and over something as old as time itself . . . a woman who doesn't really care for either of us.' She stiffened but he swept on ruthlessly: 'Kane bores you, I think. And what you feel for me is even more primitive than the way Kane and I react to each other.'

She would not shrink from the implication of the words. 'Sexual attraction? It's more than that,' she said, a little desperately, wondering how to convince him, wondering why it mattered. Certainly their relationship had been very physical from the beginning. Neither of them had wanted or expected anything more . . . and yet that was not strictly true, she suddenly discovered. She had hoped, without even knowing that she hoped, that he might come to love her as he had never loved any of those women in his past. And that argued that she had been on the threshold of loving him . . .

'Being a woman, you have to dress it up with a few fancy frills. But at least you didn't make the mistake of pretending that you love me.' His tone was harsh.

'No . . .' She smiled at him brightly. 'It isn't the rules of the game, is it? The game that you play just as well as I do . . . and we both know when it's checkmate.' She pushed open the car door, prepared to step out to the pavement. 'Bye, Paul.' With pain tearing her to pieces, she was deliberately casual. She paused to brush his cheek lightly with her lips, actress to the last. 'Thanks for the good times . . .'

She walked away from him with finality because she felt it must be the end. Obviously he did not mean to forgive the fact that she had once loved Edward who could not let her go with dignity. She could not even comfort herself with the thought that it mattered to him. For he had not given much of himself to their brief affair.

No doubt it was all for the best, she told herself with pride. For he had undoubtedly become a little too important in too short a time . . .

Paul watched her cross the pavement and wished he knew if she was as indifferent as she seemed. He did not know if he loved Miranda. He was not a believer in love. But he did not want to lose her. And that dismayed him because he had always been so independent, so self-sufficient, so easily able to cut loose and begin again with someone else. He had never wanted to be tied to any woman by his emotions. But suddenly he knew that he wanted Miranda for more than just a casual, short-lived, exciting affair, She was more important than he had supposed a woman could be to him. He needed her very much. And perhaps that was loving . . .

He was fiercely jealous of Kane. He deeply resented the fact that she had belonged to the actor before they met. It had been a severe jolt to his emotions to realise that the man still tugged at her heart. He had thought it over but her reaction to the sight of Kane in the restaurant had been unmistakable and while she might have been forewarned of his current interest in Julia Cloud, it had obviously been an unwelcome shock to see them together.

Paul believed that she did not know which of them she really wanted. Well, he had given her a choice and the freedom to make it at the very real risk of losing her. If she wanted Kane in her heart of hearts, she would certainly seize the opportunity to go back to him—knowing, as everyone must, that she would be welcomed with open arms. Paul almost envied the man his ability to stifle his pride for the sake of his happiness. For his part, he was too proud and he found it difficult to admit even to himself how much he needed Miranda.

He hoped she had outgrown her sentimental fondness for Kane and felt, as he did, that they could build successfully on the foundation of their passion for each other. He had no time for weak sentiment. He knew that sexual attraction was a very powerful force between two people and could last much longer than the idealistic emotion called love. Romantic novelists and poets and the very young might not agree with him but he knew that sex was at the root of all human relationships.

There was more than sexual attraction, too. He liked Miranda. He admired her wit and intelligence, her sense of humour, her warm and attractive personality. He enjoyed her company. He liked to show her off to his friends, delighting in her beauty and elegance and self-possession. He responded instinctively to her fierce integrity. They were friends as well as lovers and that was a new experience for a man who had always chosen his women with an eye to discarding them at the first hint of a closer relationship than he could welcome.

He hoped they would continue to be friends, to be lovers. Everything depended on Miranda. He would give her a few days to think things over and then he would certainly call her if only to learn what the future held . . .

Miranda was in a state of panic when she let herself into the empty flat. Sick and trembling, she was filled with blind, foolish panic. She had lost him. He had walked out of her life without a backward glance. Only pride and the fear that he would mock her need of him had kept her silent, forbidding her to plead with him. But now that he was gone and she did not know if she would see him again, she felt she would gladly swallow her pride.

Abruptly she pulled herself together, marvelling at her lack of self-confidence. She had never doubted her ability to hold a man in the past. And Paul was a man like any other. At the moment he was angry, smarting from that scene with Edward. When he cooled down he would know that it was madness to allow it to ruin what they had going for each other. It was a good relationship, rich and satisfying, important to them both. Paul would not let it end so unnecessarily. He simply needed a respite and he would certainly be back. If he was not . . . well, it was not the end of the world, she told herself firmly.

He was very attractive, very exciting, and she would miss him. But there was no future in such an affair and for the first time she was beginning to feel that planning for tomorrow might be just as important as living for today. She could not spend her entire life in drifting in and out of affairs with different men. She would simply end up as a lonely old woman and that thought horrified her. There was something to be said for the security of loving and caring that Edward offered . . . if he still offered it!

He was angry, too. Angry and disapproving because of her friendship with Paul that was the subject of so much gossip. He was an idealist and it had been a blow to him to discover that she was not a goddess in human form but a very ordinary woman. He was disappointed in her, of course. Perhaps that was why he had taken up with Julia Cloud.

Miranda had not met the girl before and she had been surprised to find that she was not at all like the rest of that bold, flamboyantly attractive, highly extravert family, known and loved by everyone in the profession. Julia

Cloud was a slight, insignificant, dull little creature with little to say for herself . . . not at all Edward's type!

She had been amused rather than threatened by the thought of her as a rival. She had been more disconcerted by the unexpected warmth in Paul's manner when he greeted the girl. He obviously knew her well—and liked her well! That plain, uninspiring, tongue-tied dab of a girl had brought a look to his dark eyes that Miranda had never seen for all the intimacy that they had shared. The girl must have something that appealed . . . and perhaps she had caught poor Edward on the rebound.

Yet it seemed unlikely. Edward was the faithful, eternally patient type and he loved her, Miranda thought confidently. He would wait for ever if he thought there was the smallest chance that she might go back to him—and Miranda did not rule it out entirely. If Paul really had cut her out of his life so abruptly, for instance . . .

He did not call that day nor the next. Miranda refused to wait in, sitting by the telephone. If he really wanted to get in touch, he would know where to reach her. She lunched with Jeremy Landon. She dined with another man who had been pursuing her for some time. She handled them both with consummate ease, keeping them skilfully at arms' length. She learned from friends that Edward had suffered no ill-effects from that punch-up with Paul and heard that his friendship with Julia Cloud appeared to be on the wane. She supposed that it had not pleased the little prude that Edward had fought over another woman in a public restaurant. She made her last entrance and spoke her last lines and watched the curtain fall for the last time on the ill-fated play at the *Zeus* and had a farewell drink with the rest of the cast. She left without regret although she had no work lined up. Something would come along. In the meantime, she needed a holiday. She toyed with the idea of going to Greece with Edward. Why not? Wanting Paul seemed to be an utter waste of time. Cornwall had vanished into thin air, of course . . . along with the most exciting lover she had ever known.

She missed Paul. It hurt that he could ignore her when they had been so close. She wondered if he expected or hoped that she would make a move towards renewing their affair. He was as proud as herself, after all.

On impulse, she decided to visit the club where she had first met him. He owned the place and usually made a point of calling in each night, however briefly, when he was in town. If they met by seeming chance it would not be so obvious that she was chasing him. She was chasing him, of course. She wanted him still.

She chose clothes with particular care, took special pains with her hair and face . . . and was very sure that she was looking her loveliest as she waited for him to walk in that night. She felt excited, apprehensive, desperately anxious. He was expected, she knew. He would certainly call in at some point in the evening. She would wait all night if necessary although she felt conspicuous, a woman on her own in that particular club, having to repel the inevitable advances.

Then she saw Paul, reflected in the wall mirror. Her heart turned over. The foolish heart that had been so sure it could not love, she thought wryly. He was with a very attractive woman, a careless arm about slender shoulders, a certain smile in the dark eyes that hinted at amorous intent—and, sick at heart, Miranda slipped away before he realised her presence.

As he had said, she was easily forgotten, easily replaced. No woman could mean much to him for long. Obviously he had been tiring of her and seized on a ridiculously slight excuse to end their affair.

He did not care at all. She had always known it so why did her heart feel that it was being slowly torn into small pieces. He was no good, she knew. He was too selfish, too sensual, a care for nobody. She did not always like him. But how was she to live without him? Paul, Paul . . . how could she bear the terrible emptiness, day after day? The utter meaningless of life that had no purpose?

Had Edward felt like this, she wondered. Her heart went out to him in compassion. Poor Edward. Poor Miranda . . .

Of all the men in the world that she might have loved, it had to be Paul Keller. A man who was incapable of loving. A man who lived only for the pleasure of the moment. A man entirely without heart, without pity, without conscience. A man who did not deserve to be loved as she loved him, she thought bleakly, wondering why no one had ever warned her that loving hurt so much.

She did not know what to do. The bottom had suddenly fallen out of her world. She had been so sure that Paul would come back, needing her as she needed him if he could not love her. His silence had not really disturbed or alarmed her after those first moments of panic. She knew herself to be beautiful, desirable, much sought after by men . . . and Paul would not let her go so easily. He had known a very real passion for her. She had refused to believe it could be quenched so swiftly. He would be back and she would not reproach him by so much as a word or a look for she understood how much he hated any hint of possessiveness. She had always hated it herself. Now she longed for Paul to care enough to want to keep her close, to guard her jealously, to insist that she must belong to him for always.

He had not come back. He had found

another woman as easily as he always did and Miranda was filled with fierce hatred of a stranger who had smiled on him with invitation. The thought of someone else in his arms, knowing his kisses, his touch, the urgency of his passion drove her to desperation . . . and in desperation she found herself hailing a taxi and giving the driver the address of the little house in Harrow where she would find Edward.

He loved her. He was not Paul but he was kind and generous and warm-hearted, thoughtful and considerate and caring—and he loved her. Paul had merely used her until she bored him and then gone with scarcely a goodbye. Paul was a madness, a fever in the blood, a terrible bondage that threatened to hold her more fast than any marriage vow. She might marry Edward but she would belong for the rest of her life to a man who would never truly give himself to any woman . . .

CHAPTER EIGHT

Edward knew immediately that someone was in the house. And only Miranda, apart from himself, had a key.

He walked into the sitting-room. She was curled in an armchair, waiting for him. Edward looked at her without surprise, without delight.

It was ironic that her confident and very lovely smile should announce her return now that he had discovered that he did not want her back. Only a few days before he would have been over the moon with relief and thankfulness.

Now he felt absolutely nothing. Even her beauty did not stir him. It was strange when he had prayed for weeks that she would come back, had lived with the constant hope that she would regret leaving him. He wondered what brought her back now that it was too late. His heart did not leap with the hope that she loved him, after all. His heart was entirely his own again and he was glad of it. Loving was hell and he wanted no more of it!

'Hi . . .' he said slowly.

Miranda was satisfied although he had not shouted with joy or swept her into his arms. He had simply accepted her presence as the most natural thing in the world and that made things easy. She might never have been away.

'I'll get you a drink,' she said lightly and rose to her feet.

Edward nodded, tossed his jacket over a chair. 'I could use one.' He sat down and ran a hand over his eyes, yawning. He was very tired.

Miranda brought his drink. His head was thrown back, his eyes closed. She looked down at him with tenderness. He looked very young, very vulnerable. She was suddenly aware that she was really very fond of him. Perhaps it would not be such a bad thing to marry him, spend the rest of her life with him. She might even find it possible to stop wanting Paul . . . one day, when she was very, very old.

Gently she touched her fingers to the faint bruise on his jaw. Edward opened his eyes and looked at her dispassionately. She felt a flicker of apprehension. He was very distant. Not cold or hostile or contemptuous. Just distant. They might be strangers. But he must love her still, want her still! She needed him, now more than ever!

She smiled into his unsmiling eyes. 'Dear Edward,' she said softly. She knelt by his chair and reached for his hands but found no instant, answering pressure. She kissed him and his lips were cold, unwilling to respond. She had taken his love and his need for granted all these weeks. She would not believe that suddenly they did not exist. She kissed him again.

Edward sighed. A few days before, he would have been the happiest of men to find her waiting for him when he came home, ready to forget the past and begin again. But things had changed. He had not thought it possible that he could cease to love her. But he had. He had been so sure that his love was for a lifetime. But he had suddenly, painfully, discovered that the woman he loved did not really exist. He had fallen under the spell of her beauty and endowed her with all the qualities he wanted in a woman, blinding himself to the truth that he loved the woman he wished her to be and not the woman that she was. The real Miranda was cold and calculating and she used people. She had allowed him to love her while it suited her and she had not hesitated to hurt him when she became restless, wanting more than he could give. She had used him. Now she wanted to use him again. Keller had probably let her down and she had turned back to him in the confident certainty that he would be waiting. He could not blame her for that, remembering how he had sworn to love her always, assured her that he would always want her, begged her to come back to him again and again. She would not understand any more than he did that all that loving could suddenly die on him.

He put her away from him, a little abruptly. 'What about Keller?' He was not really interested but he felt that she expected him to ask the question.

She was silent for a moment. Then she smiled warmly, reassuringly. 'I won't be seeing him again.'

The man had tired of her, of course. As he tired of every woman. Miranda had been foolish to suppose that she could succeed where all the others had failed. 'That was inevitable.'

'I daresay.' She managed a slight shrug of her shoulders, a display of indifference. 'Some things aren't meant to last.'

The words were an echo. He remembered with a sudden, totally unexpected pang that Julia had said much the same thing with a haunting sadness in her eyes.

He had not blamed her for deciding that she did not want to see him again. Then, still smarting from the humiliation of his encounter with Keller and too angry to think kindly of any woman and least of all Miranda, he had parted with Julia with careless unconcern. From the beginning, his liking for her had been tinged with slight guilt. He had felt that he was using her as a weapon to punish Miranda who did not really interest herself in his affairs any more. He had not been fair to Julia who had fallen so swiftly in love. He had given her so little. Julia. Sweet and warm and wonderful, loving and giving with all her heart. A flood of memories tugged at him and he knew that his brief friendship with her had meant a different kind of happiness. Something rare and very precious . . .

'When it's right, it lasts for ever,' he said quietly, finally accepting that his love for Miranda had been real enough but lacking in the rightness that could have bound him to her for eternity. *When the right one comes along . . .* He had laughed at the tag but now he understood its meaning.

Miranda had not been right for him any more than he had been truly right for her. The kind of love they had known for each other had not been meant to last. He had been too demanding, too posessive—and she had been too insistent on going her own way.

'You won't be seeing me again, either.' The words were harsh but his tone was very gentle, letting her down lightly.

Miranda sat back on her heels, staring at him. 'What did you say?' She knew perfectly well but she could not believe it. It was not possible that Edward was turning her down!

'I mean it, Miranda.'

'I came back to marry you,' she said, a little desperately.

'I expect you'd rather go to Cornwall with Keller,' he said quietly.

'No . . . !' She was just a little too vehement.

He smiled with understanding. 'Trying to atone? Or out to make Keller wish he hadn't parted with you? You don't really want to marry me, you know.'

'Yes, I do! We'll go to Greece for our honeymoon just as you've always wanted. I'll make you so happy, Edward. I'll be just the kind of wife you want!'

'For how long? You couldn't keep it up, Miranda. Six months and you'd be falling into the arms of another Keller just to escape from the boredom of being the kind of wife I want.'

She was shaken but unable to accept that a man who had loved so much could have ceased to care quite so completely. Something must remain. Suddenly he had discovered his pride

. . . a little late in the day, she thought ruefully. Well, she had not expected it to be easy after that fracas at the *Caprice*.

'All right, Edward. We won't talk of marriage for the time being,' she said, getting to her feet. She smiled at him warmly. 'But I do want to come back. I *am* back, darling . . . asking you to forgive and forget.'

He looked at her for a long moment. 'Go home, Miranda,' he said gently.

'Edward . . . !'

He kissed her lightly on the brow. 'Go home and make it up with Keller. Or find another Keller. We aren't right for each other, you know.'

'You're angry, bitter. It's very natural that you should be when I've behaved so wrongly, so stupidly. But revenge—no, that isn't like you, Edward,' she said slowly, clinging to straws.

'I want you to be happy. Does that seem like revenge?'

'I shall be happy with you,' she persisted.

'Happy with someone who doesn't love you? I know you better than you seem to know yourself,' he said wryly. 'You must be loved, Miranda. I don't think it's in you to love.'

He did not mean to be cruel, she knew. But the words stabbed viciously at a heart that seemed to be slowly bleeding to death. 'You are mistaken,' she said quietly.

He was swift to catch the inflection of pain,

despair. He was equally swift to understand and sympathise. 'Keller?' he asked, knowing the answer and thankful to confirm his new awareness that it no longer mattered if she loved someone else. 'He's hurt you—and you came running to me to kiss it better. I wish it were possible . . .' He put an arm about her shoulders, hugged her to him. 'I'm sorry. I know about hurt.'

'Yes.' She put a hand to his cheek. 'I'm sorry, too.' She sighed. 'You're right. I shouldn't have come here. But you always gave so much, Edward. You have too good a heart. It's a great temptation for an unscrupulous woman.'

'You've always been straight with me,' he said firmly.

'Until tonight.' She sighed. 'I don't think I knew what I was doing. I seem to have lost my way. It isn't a nice feeling . . .'

She drove home, slowly, trying to straighten her thoughts, marshal her emotions. She supposed she was thankful that Edward had sent her away, no longer wanted her—but it had been a blow she had not foreseen. Even Edward! She would have staked her life on his loyalty, she thought with a touch of bitterness. But his love had not lasted for all his passionate declarations. She supposed he had found consolation in the arms of Julia Cloud. Well, she hoped he would be happy. As for herself . . . real and lasting happiness seemed to be always just out of reach.

What was it about her that men could not love her as she needed so desperately to be loved? Why did they tire so quickly like Paul— or undergo an eventual change of heart like Edward? What was lacking in her that she was destined to drift from man to man, meaning little to any of them, being disappointed in each of them?

A long white car stood outside the entrance of the tall building that housed her luxurious flat. Miranda stared with incredulous and delighted relief for she could not fail to recognise the personalised number plate. She was suddenly very thankful that Edward had sent her away so unexpectedly. For if Paul had waited in vain for her that night he would have realised that she was with Edward and it would certainly have been the end of everything between them. For he had told her too many times that he would not share her with any man.

With a tumultuous heart, she pushed through the swing doors into the entrance hall. Paul turned from his conversation with the night porter and came towards her. 'You keep late hours,' he drawled.

Miranda wanted to hurl herself into his arms. She was so thankful to see him and surely his presence proved that he had wanted very much to see her! His reasons did not matter in that moment. But she was still unable to humble herself so utterly in her need of any man, still reluctant to give herself so completely to the kind of loving that he seemed to inspire.

'No one waits up for me,' she returned coolly, walking towards the lift. 'An advantage of being single is that I may please myself what time I come in at night.'

'Outweighed by the disadvantage of a cold and lonely bed,' he suggested lightly.

'I may please myself about that, too.' Her tone was tart.

His eyes twinkled, 'Lovers have no rights,' he agreed. 'A husband might insist on sharing your bed.'

Miranda summoned the lift. 'Did you call in for a friendly chat with the night porter? Or were you actually waiting for me?'

'You didn't expect me?'

'No.'

He raised an eyebrow. 'Didn't you wish to see me? Gerry said you were at the club earlier tonight, asking for me.' His careless tone did not betray the glow of satisfaction he had felt at the piece of information.

'And of course you came running,' she said drily.

'Of course.'

'I thought you'd have more on your mind than me,' she said, a little drily. 'I hope you didn't disappoint the lady for my sake.'

He followed her into the lift, pressed the

button for her floor. 'So you saw me with Iris? I doubt if you were surprised,' he said carelessly. 'You know that I like to have a woman in tow.'

'Any woman,' she commented sweetly.

'One woman is much like another,' he agreed smoothly.

It was exactly what she expected from him. But it hurt, nevertheless—and all the more because she had no way of knowing if he was really so cold, so cavalier in his attitude to all women including herself. She searched for her doorkey as the lift stopped at the fourth floor. 'I suppose you mean to come in?' Her tone did not offer an invitation.

He smiled. 'I haven't waited half the night for you only to be dismissed on the doorstep, my dear.'

'Very well. But you aren't staying,' she said with finality. 'I won't be picked up and put down as the fancy takes you, Paul.'

'Don't you credit me with any finer feelings?' he demanded, amused.

'None at all.' She opened the door and led the way into the sitting-room. She laid her bag and wrap on a chair. 'Do you want a drink?'

'Not if you really mean to send me away. I'm driving,' he reminded her lightly. He reached for her, drew her close, smiled into the sapphire eyes with warm intent. 'Do you . . .?'

Miranda was aware of carefully-controlled passion beneath the superficial lightness and she wondered bleakly if only a persistent desire for her had brought him that night. Sexual rapport had been strong between them from the very beginning and her own wanting leaped instantly at his touch. Yet she knew she could not lie happily in his arms, loving him and knowing how little he really cared about her, how carelessly he would move on to the next woman if she resisted him. She wondered if she had the strength and the courage to say no to him—and if she could afford to run the risk of losing him entirely. He had come back, quite unexpectedly and unpredictably. She could not send him away again . . .

He kissed her, long and lingering and wholly sensuous. He heard the soft, sighing intake of her breath and was satisfied that she still wanted him just as fiercely as he wanted her. But she was as proud and stubborn as himself and she would not yield to loving. Perhaps she was wise. He had never known any lasting good to come of the foolish fancy that man called love. Primitive passion was eternal. Loving was ephemeral . . .

All desire slaked, he slept. Miranda raised herself from the pillows to look at him in the early light of the morning and she touched her lips almost reverently to the broad column of his throat. Her heart welled within her abruptly. She had never experienced such an intensity of emotion as he could evoke. It frightened her just a little. Her need of him was almost obsessive and certainly possessive . . . and she had always been so convinced that no man could humble her to that extent!

She loved him and she wanted to spend the rest of her life with him and she knew there could be no happiness for her without him. But Paul Keller was a man who had no heart for loving and no stomach for marriage, she thought bleakly. She understood because such a short time before she had been exactly the same, taking without a thought for giving and utterly indifferent to any hurt she might inflict on a hopeful heart. But all the understanding in the world did not ease the despair she felt that Paul's continued need of her was born of passion rather than real loving.

However, they were together once more— and those few days without him had been empty and seemingly endless, emphasising his importance in her life. She must accept with a good grace the little that he offered and take care not to let him know that she yearned for so much more. Because he was the kind of man to draw back from the least hint of a loving he could not welcome . . .

CHAPTER NINE

Miranda fell in love with Penmawr at first sight. The lovely old house in its graceful setting was a gem of rare beauty. Its welcoming atmosphere made her feel immediately at home and she understood Paul's obvious affection for the place.

She slipped a hand into his arm as they stood on the stone terrace that overlooked the spacious well-kept gardens. 'It's a happy house, Paul,' she said warmly.

He smiled down at her. 'Yes, I think so.'

Miranda was happy in that moment. He was relaxed, looking younger than she had yet seen him, and there was a new and reassuring warmth in his dark eyes. Her heart lifted with hope. Perhaps here, in these quiet and peaceful and very lovely surroundings, he would come to love her as she loved him. Certainly they had every opportunity to get to know each other thoroughly.

Penmawr was close to the sea. A little path led down to the quiet, sandy cove tucked so neatly between the rugged rocks that few people knew of its existence. The house was some distance from its nearest neighbours. The village was almost two miles away along the coast. Paul was ensured the privacy and the peace that was so necessary to him when he contrived to snatch a few days from the many demands of his business interests.

He was a very wealthy man. Miranda had not realised the extent of his wealth until he flew her to Cornwall in his private plane, a Cessna, and she saw Penmawr in its lovely grounds complete with tennis courts and swimming-pool and miniature golf course. She could not fail to be impressed. It was not surprising that he was considered a very eligible catch despite a reputation that ought to frighten the hopeful mothers of marriageable daughters, she thought drily. And, unlike some eligible men that she knew, he was extremely attractive and very personable and much too easy to love. She could well believe that he had left a string of broken hearts in his wake. She was terribly afraid that her own heart was at risk . . .

For three days, they were alone except for the staff of the big house. They were long, idyllic days despite the soft rain that fell so persistently. They walked in the rain, hand in hand . . . on the beach, along the cliffs, down to the village so that he could show her the beauty of the old church where lay the original owners of Penmawr and their descendants.

They drove for miles through the Cornish countryside, exploring places that Paul had never seen for all the years that he had owned Penmawr. They swam in a sea that was surprisingly warm and lay on the sand in the shelter of a small cave that time and tide had eroded beneath the rocky cliff.

They talked of books and art and music and theatre, Miranda sitting at his feet before the cheerful fire that was lighted not because it was cold but because it created a pleasing homeliness in the big and beautifully furnished sitting-room. He played for her on the superb Bechstein, so beautifully that tears rolled down her cheeks. They listened together in the comfortable intimacy of silence to music that both loved, discovering that they shared many favourites.

They talked and kissed and laughed and made love and laughed again as lovers should. Miranda was very happy, falling more and more deeply in love with the man who had so many facets to his unusual personality.

Paul was happy, too. Relaxed and restored, he delighted in her beauty, her quick wit, her gaiety, her readiness to please and be pleased and her eager response to his lovemaking. She was a delightful companion and an enchanting lover. He was beginning to feel that loving, if it was mutual, might have something in its favour, after all. But, while Miranda was obviously pleased to be with him, happy in his company and ecstatic in his embrace, he did not think she loved him and she was much too honest to pretend. In his experience, a woman in love could not keep it to herself and not one word of love had ever escaped Miranda even at the height of the passion they shared.

It was a pity that the idyll had to end . . .

A party of his friends arrived on Friday for the weekend. Too many of them for Miranda's liking. She had undoubtedly been spoiled during those few days when she had known his undivided attention.

Now she had to share him . . . and it became obvious very quickly that her share was going to be very small.

At dinner that first night, she looked around the long table. She knew two of the guests slightly, Henry and Lucilla Tremayne, the only married couple. Henry threatened to be too attentive and Lucilla was a first-class bitch.

The rest were strangers who did not seem unduly anxious to be friends. Four men, four women. She knew instinctively that the women disliked and resented her intimacy with Paul. Their amused patronage and light-hearted rivalry made her feel like a very unimportant newcomer to the long list of his conquests. They implied by subtle and not-so-subtle means that she was far from the first and not at all likely to be the last of his women. They also paraded the amorous interludes they had enjoyed with Paul in the past and hinted that he would be more than ready to pick up old threads if any one of them offered encouragement.

Miranda knew his reputation, his off-with-the-old and on-with-the-new fickleness, his careless disregard for convention or even acceptable behaviour. But she clung to the hope that something more than sexual attraction drew him to her and she hugged to her hopeful heart the memory of the golden days they had just shared. Could any one of these women have glimpsed the secret corners of his heart and mind as she had? Could any one of them have known such memorable moments, such rare raptures with him? Could any one of them have meant as much to him as she must believe that she did?

Her gaze rested on Paul for a long moment. He was laughing . . . very attractive, entirely endearing. Her heart welled with love for him and she wished he would send her one swift, reassuring glance to show that she was not forgotten for his friends.

The woman by his side was very beautiful. Miranda had seen her before . . . once. With Paul. His arm about her shoulders, a warm glow in his dark eyes, a certain smile curving his lips. Iris Woodley was a widow in her late twenties, a well-known and very successful fashion model. Dark of hair and eye with superb skin and a warm smile and the elegant slenderness that was so much admired, she was a very vivacious and attractive person. It would not be surprising if Paul was attracted, Miranda thought bleakly. Such a sensual man would respond instinctively to the sexual appeal of a woman like Iris Woodley.

Her husband had been Cy Woodley, the famous financier who had died of a heart attack earlier in the year. He had been Paul's friend, apparently—and Miranda did not doubt that Iris was using the fact of that friendship to her own ends.

Listening to the easy, amused banter that passed around and across the table, she discovered that Iris meant to marry Paul before the year was out. It was said in jest and treated as such by everyone but Miranda who found it totally unamusing. She did not think that Iris was joking—and her smiling confidence implied that Paul had given her cause to believe it not only possible but likely.

He was attentive, obviously fond of the woman. Perhaps he did mean to marry her, Miranda thought bleakly. A man like Paul would probably choose a wife for very different reasons to those that prompted his choice of mistress. But if so, why had he invited Iris to Penmawr at the same time as he was entertaining her, Miranda wondered, almost angrily. To emphasise that she had no hope of marrying him if that was her ambition? One never knew with a man like Paul.

It was an uncomfortable evening. She did not feel at ease with his friends and she was disinclined to make much effort to be pleasant to them. It was not her place to entertain them, after all, she thought crossly, resenting

106

their very presence. She had not been invited to Penmawr to play hostess. That would be a very different matter, a compliment and an indication that she was more than just another of his many mistresses.

She felt that his friends viewed her with amused contempt. With their arrival, she was pushed into a very insignificant corner of the stage and Paul made no attempt to draw her back into the limelight, she thought angrily. She wondered if he gave any thought to her at all as he talked and laughed and enjoyed himself with his friends.

Paul did think about her, of course . . . with irritation and disappointment. He had looked forward to showing her off to his friends and it was exasperating that she was behaving as petulantly as a spoiled child because she no longer had his full attention.

She snubbed Henry Tremayne when he ventured to sit beside her and begin a conversation. She smiled coldly and shook her head when Richard Pooley invited her to play backgammon. She refused to be drawn into girl-talk with Lucilla Tremayne and Ann Madison. She walked out to the terrace in obvious pique when he danced with Marian Gilmore to the music from the stereo.

He followed at the first moment that offered, frowning, disliking the amused exchange of glances between his friends because he was obliged to soothe the obviously ruffled feathers of the new woman in his life. He was a very proud man and he was annoyed with Miranda for putting him in such a position.

Miranda felt sick with jealousy, with regret that the delight of the last days had been shadowed, with the bleak conviction that Paul had never come near to loving her at all. Nothing could be less lover-like or more humiliating than his neglect before the friends who were so ready to think her of little account.

She turned to find him regarding her, unsmiling, forbidding. She went to him swiftly with a swishing swirl of her long skirts, smiling to conceal the dismay and apprehension that she felt. 'It's a lovely night,' she said softly. 'Have you come out to enjoy it with me?'

She either did not know or simply did not care that she had offended, he thought grimly. 'I'm in no mood to enjoy anything with you,' he said quietly but with anger. 'I want an explanation, Miranda. You've embarrassed my friends and offended me with your petulant behaviour, your ridiculous jealousy. Do you think that you own me?'

She bit her lip. But all the hurt could not prevent her temper from rising at the injustice of his words. 'I don't like your friends,' she said bluntly. 'The men try to paw me and the women only want to score off me. I'm sorry if that offends you but I have to be honest.'

His eyes flashed. 'Don't cloak deliberate rudeness with an aura of honesty. It only makes matters worse,' he said coldly. 'You haven't made the slightest effort to like my friends or to be pleasant to them. You've behaved like a jealous prima donna since they arrived. Frankly, I'm astonished. I wonder how I conveyed the impression that you have the right to parade your demands.' Angry, he struck to hurt. 'Women are all the same . . . give them a little and they begin to think they own a man body and soul! But I thought you were different, Miranda. You disappoint me.'

Colour fled from her face and her heart swelled. Near to tears, she flew at him angrily: 'Damn you! You disappoint me, too. I've given you more than a little and you reward me with less attention than you'd grant a casual acquaintance! And you cheapen our relationship by allowing those bitches to treat me as a nothing!' It was unreasonable but a woman in love cannot be expected to think logically or to weigh her words when she feels that her happiness is threatened.

He looked down at her without liking. 'I suggest you go to bed and take your tantrum with you. I'll make your excuses—a headache, I think. That will account for your sulky behaviour—and in the morning you'll be all smiles and as charming as you know how to be!' His tone was harsh, autocratic.

Her chin tilted. 'Telling me how to behave,

Paul?' she demanded ominously.

'Telling you!' he said sharply. 'And regretting the necessity for it!' He spun on his heel and strode away from her . . . more dismayed than angry.

Nothing had led him to suppose that she could be so unreasonable, so foolish, so irritatingly feminine. She must know that he owed much of his attention to people he liked and admired and had known for a long time, people who were his guests. She had every right to dislike where she pleased, of course . . . no right whatsoever to show that dislike beneath his roof!

He was deeply disappointed. He did not consider that he had neglected her. It seemed to him that he had behaved as a husband might in such circumstances, expecting his wife to play her part in entertaining their guests and understand that he could not dance attendance upon her like a lover. He had been aware of her at all times—and that was more than most women had been granted in the past.

Her attitude was wholly unexpected and quite unjustified when he had spent the last few days in proving his affection and desire and need for her, he thought with sudden anger. He was puzzled by the jealousy she evinced when he did not believe that she was at all in love with him.

Women were the very devil, he told himself

110

wryly. But he had been ready to endow Miranda with certain qualities that the women in his past had lacked. He had been near to loving her, in fact. Now he hesitated, drew back, knew again the wisdom of refusing to commit himself so irrevocably. Not even Miranda should have the power to rule his life with her smiles or frowns.

And to prove it to himself as well as to his friends, he flirted recklessly with Marian Gilmore, allowed himself to respond to the near-embrace of Lucilla Tremayne as they danced, devoted himself to ensuring the enjoyment of the lovely and very appealing Iris Woodley—and only wished that Miranda could be present to realise how foolish it was to alienate him with the possessive jealousy that had ruined so many of his relationships with women.

Later that night, Paul went along the corridor to have a quiet word with Iris in her room. She had some documents to discuss with him. She had been heavily burdened by Cy's untimely death and she struggled gamely to cope with business details. Paul acted as adviser on many matters and they were very good friends. He valued her affection, enjoyed her company. Too much pursued by women, it was a relief to be with Iris who made no demands on him.

She welcomed him with a smile, indicating the drink that was ready for him on a table beside a comfortable chair. 'A nightcap, Paul.'

He sat down, smiling. 'This is nice,' he said warmly. 'It's good to be with you, Iris.' Still smarting from Miranda's unaccountable behaviour, he felt soothed by Iris's easy, undemanding warmth. He knew exactly where he was with Iris, he felt thankfully.

Smiling, she touched her lips lightly to his dark hair as she moved behind him to sit down in the opposite chair. 'It's good to be with you too,' she said with easy affection. She indicated the folder on the table between them. 'The papers I spoke about . . . but you needn't read through them now, of course. Take them with you.' She sipped her drink. 'How is Miranda now?' She did not attempt to pretend that she was ignorant of the intimacy between them.

He frowned. 'Asleep, I expect.'

'You treat your women abominably,' she said lightly. 'I'm not surprised that she was so upset.'

He raised an eyebrow. 'What did I do?'

She laughed softly. 'It's what you don't do, my dear. You can be so hurtfully casual. I should hate it myself. Women like the world to know when a man is in love with them, Paul. You lean over backwards to make it seem that there's nothing more to your interest in any woman than the sex thing.'

'I'm not in love with Miranda,' he said almost curtly.

'I know it. Does she?' she asked gently.

'We understand each other. I don't set out to break hearts, Iris,' he said carelessly. 'She doesn't love me, either. It's entirely a sex thing, as you call it.' There was a hint of harshness in his tone.

'Clever Paul,' she teased, smiling. 'How do you dissuade your women from loving you when you are so utterly fascinating?'

He laughed, amused. 'Do you want to find out?' It was a joke, not to be taken seriously, much like the little game they often played before their friends.

So was her light-hearted reply. 'It wouldn't work, Paul. You see, I love you already . . .'

CHAPTER TEN

Miranda's mind and heart were in turmoil. That stupid quarrel, for which she was ready to blame herself entirely, had alarmed and appalled her. What was she about to quarrel with Paul? Was she so sure of him that she could afford to cross swords with him, risk offending him beyond forgiveness?

She waited for him for a seeming eternity, refusing to believe that he would not come to her. She was anxious to apologise, to make amends, to do anything to dispel that hurtful coldness between them. At last, she heard voices in the corridor, the opening and closing of doors, the indications that everyone was retiring to their rooms.

She waited for a few more minutes, her heart pounding. But the communicating door between their rooms remained ominously shut. She strained her ears for some sound that would indicate his presence in the adjoining room. There was none.

She rose from the bed, drawing the cream lace negligee more tightly about her slender body, her heart beating heavily in her throat. She tapped lightly on the communicating door and entered his room, praying he would not rebuff her. The room was empty. His dinner jacket was on a chair, silent witness that he had been in and partially undressed before leaving again.

Miranda's hands clenched convulsively. Where was he? With whom? Her mind shrank instinctively from the image that presented itself. He would not humiliate her so! Yet when had Paul Keller ever hesitated to take what he wanted without a thought for anything but his own sensual desires, she thought bitterly, trying to hate him, knowing that she could not cease to love him.

Despising herself, she slipped out into the corridor, moved quietly along to the door of Iris Woodley's bedroom and paused, listening with an agitated heart. She heard the murmur of voices, one unmistakably Paul's . . . and his deep, attractive laugh.

Sick at heart, she went back to her own room. Throwing herself on the bed, she cried as she had never cried in her life. Miranda Lynch, who did not believe that anything was bad enough for the contemptuous weakness of tears! Miranda Lynch, who was so confidently in command of every situation! Miranda Lynch, whose heart had always been so completely her own . . . until she met and loved Paul Keller.

Loving him, she wept for the happiness she would never know with him, the future she would never share with him. Loving him, she knew that he did not love her, would never love her—and she was filled with despair and desperation.

She heard him return to his room at last—centuries later, it seemed. She buried her face in the pillows so that he should not hear the sobs that racked her still. She could not bear him to know that he was breaking her heart with his casual need, his careless indifference to her feelings.

She did not sleep at all. The new day dawned with brilliant sunshine and blue skies and the promise of heat. It was a golden dawn to emphasise the heavy lead of the heart in her breast, she thought unhappily.

She was at the window, indifferently watching the antics of some early risers who were cavorting in the pool, when Paul came into her room. She did not turn, unable to trust herself to smile without betraying her hurt.

He looked at the slim, uncompromising back. Was she still sulking? Angry with him because he had not sought her embrace in the night, patching up that silly quarrel between lovers? He might have done so but he had spent longer than he intended with Iris, talking about Cy and the old days. He told himself firmly that lovers did not need to be forever locked in each other's arms—and if they did then something was lacking in the relationship.

'Good morning,' he said smoothly, willing to overlook her strange behaviour of the previous evening if she responded to him now with warm friendliness. Women were moody creatures, after all.

She glanced at him, moved from the window and went to the dressing-table where she took up her brush and began to pull it through her thick curls. 'Sleep well?' she asked with an edge to her voice.

'Very well.' A little smile played about his mouth. Did she imagine that he had lost sleep over her tantrum and jealousy? Or did she suppose that he had spent a restless night, missing her embrace?

'Sign of an easy conscience.' She looked at him through the cascade of her gleaming hair. 'Or no conscience at all.'

He laughed. 'Men with consciences are usually very dull, don't you find?'

116

'Dull predictability is beginning to seem very attractive,' she returned tartly, sweeping her hair from her face and briskly knotting it on the nape of her neck, securing it with a handful of hairpins.

'I detect a note of nostalgia for the halcyon days with Edward,' he said mockingly.

'I daresay you might!'

'Miss him, do you?'

'Yes, I do,' she said with truth. Edward had been reliable, trustworthy, kind and considerate. It seemed to her that Paul Keller was none of those things and it had been madness to become involved with him. Edward would never have treated her in such cruel, cavalier fashion, she thought ruefully . . . and wondered at that streak of perversity in her nature which insisted that she loved the man who did.

Paul's eyes narrowed at the words and their obvious sincerity. Did she care for Kane and learned it too late, having lost him to endearing Julia Cloud with her warm heart and sweet nature? Was that the reason for her inability to give him her heart as well as her body? Paul did not want to be loved. It was a complication and an unwelcome responsibility. But it did not please him that when she lay in his arms she might be longing for Kane!

He put an arm about her waist, drawing her close. She resisted him slightly. He smiled, the slow, mocking smile that she had learned to dread, and said lightly: 'Will you miss me, too, Miranda?'

Her heart plunged. The implication was unmistakable. But her chin tilted with pride and her eyes were bright with amused indifference as she returned with equal lightness: 'As much as you'll miss me, I daresay.'

'Not at all then,' he drawled.

'Not at all,' she agreed, smiling, her world collapsing about her at the mere thought of losing him.

'I knew you were my kind of woman,' he said smoothly. He bent to kiss her but she turned her head. 'Kiss me!' he said with sudden sharpness.

'Not on an empty stomach!' she retorted, taking refuge in flippancy. She could not endure the touch of his lips, she thought desperately. She might cling to him weakly, without pride. She might humble herself utterly in the need to keep him. She might betray the aching, despairing love for him that possessed her so completely, far transcending and yet encompassing the sexual rapport that had first brought them together.

Paul laughed softly. 'Must I make you . . .?' he demanded, low and urgent, a little glow in his dark eyes, his arms tightening about the beautiful, sensuous body that always responded to him so readily. Desire for her was suddenly fierce, compelling.

Miranda quickened at the look in his eyes. He wanted her, she knew . . . this man who was so utterly and hurtfully sensual. And she wanted him. With heart and soul and body, now and forever. She slid her arms about his neck and raised her face for his kiss and something that was half-sigh, half-sob escaped her at the first touch of his urgent lips. She had no pride, she thought weakly. She knew he had lain in another woman's arms only a few hours earlier and she ought to reject him in pride and anger and loathing. But his touch, his kiss, his very nearness filled her with a wanting that would not be denied . . .

Paul was disturbed by the intensity of emotion that consumed him, so much greater than anything he had experienced in the past. Passion was not new to him but it was a different kind of fire that leaped when he took her in his arms, he discovered. Sexual need mingled with other needs that he had not known he possessed until he met Miranda and fell under the spell of her loveliness, her charm, her warm and exciting and challenging personality.

The emotion she evoked was new and very disconcerting. It threatened to leap out of control and it was the first time that he had not been able to handle an affair with easy confidence in its outcome. Could he keep Miranda? Did he want to? Was he beginning to make the kind of demands on her that he had always resisted himself? Did he want her to love him . . . or did he merely resent playing second fiddle to Kane? Was he falling in love with her for all his resistance to the very idea?

He drew the pins from her hair, one by one. The lovely mass of curls tumbled on the pillow, gold in the bright sunlight that streamed through the window. She was beautiful, quite enchantingly lovely, a smile in the sapphire eyes, the luminous softness of loving still touching her oval face with glowing radiance. Paul felt an odd little contraction of his heart, an aching tenderness, an unexpected wave of warmth and longing that owed nothing whatsoever to the sexual delights they had just shared.

Foolish little phrases came unbidden to mind . . . words used by lovers and poets throughout the ages. *My love is like a red, red rose. My heart's delight. Dearest dear. My ain true love. My love, my life, my all. I love you.* The last and simplest of them all were the hardest in the world for a man like himself to utter, he found—and was afraid to trust the surge of sentiment.

Love was too much of a threat to a man who enjoyed and valued his freedom. And love that might be rejected because he was not Edward Kane or anything like him was totally unacceptable to a proud and sensitive man.

He kissed her briefly, very lightly. 'Time for breakfast . . .'

'Paul . . .' She held him fast, trying to recapture the magic. Something very fragile and lovely and vital had seemed just within her grasp. Surely they had been closer in that moment than ever before? Surely there had been new meaning in his gaze, his touch, that hint of a kiss? Surely a real and mutual love had vibrated between them for a precious moment?

'Let me go, woman!' he commanded lightly. But he smiled into her eyes and kissed her again with a lingering tenderness that filled her heart with tremulous hope.

It was swiftly shattered. She went down to breakfast and found him and Iris Woodley with their heads together in obvious intimacy. Iris looked up and smiled and greeted her with pleasant warmth . . . and Miranda knew that the smile ill-concealed a mocking triumph. She tried not to think of her in Paul's arms but it was far from easy. For the first time in her life she knew what it meant to hate and it took all her resolution to respond with even a modicum of civility.

Her dislike was so patent and so unjustified that Paul was annoyed, sensitive to Iris's hurt at being snubbed when she was doing her best to offer friendship. Miranda was so jealous, so resentful of losing any of his attention, that she was as prickly as a hedgehog and it irked him that his friends were obviously wondering at his continued interest in a woman who made such demands on him.

He wondered at it, too. He knew many beautiful women . . . just as attractive, as desirable, as delightful as Miranda. What extra something did she have that held him so firmly? What was it that made him so reluctant to part with her even though he loathed the possessiveness she was displaying so unexpectedly?

He had been deeply disturbed by the mood of the morning, that strange intensity of emotion that had shattered all his preconceived ideas of loving. He was still reluctant to admit that he loved. He needed time to think, to be very sure, before he committed himself so irrevocably to any woman. Miranda meant very much to him, obviously. His need for her went deeper than anything he had previously experienced. But a love that could last for a lifetime? He did not know . . . and a natural caution kept him from declaring that it was love he felt for a woman who might never love him . . .

He was still master of himself. He could put the problem of Miranda and the future to the back of his mind and concentrate on entertaining his friends. He could enjoy the day, swimming and sunbathing, playing tennis and golf, strolling in the grounds, exchanging lazy banter as well as turning his mind to serious topics. He was not surprised to discover that Miranda made no effort to endear herself to people she was determined not to like. Proud and stubborn and wilful, she went her own way at the risk of incurring his displeasure all over again, he thought wryly. He understood because she was so much like himself . . . but it was disappointing that she did not care enough for him to wish to please him in the matter of his friends.

He studied her more in sorrow than in anger that evening as she riffled idly through a magazine, taking no part in the conversation that went on around her. She was aloof, disdainful, barely polite and very bored . . . and her attitude was spoiling the weekend for him and everyone else!

Iris paused by his chair and laid a hand lightly on his shoulder. He looked up swiftly, smiling . . . and raised his hand to cover her slender fingers in a gesture of affection. She was very dear . . . and reassuringly undemanding. Perhaps he was a fool to go on wanting Miranda who was proving to be a torment rather than a delight. Perhaps there was something to be said for settling down with one woman—and not necessarily someone who stirred his blood like the sensual but wholly unsentimental Miranda. She loved with passion but without heart. Iris was all heart, warm and sympathetic and very generous with her affections. She had been a good and loving wife to his friend. Paul was far from committed to the idea of marriage but he toyed with it. He had promised Cy to look after Iris and a man might be happier with her, if he chose to marry, than with someone whose resistance to loving matched his own. Miranda would probably refuse to marry him if he was fool enough to ask her, anyway . . .

Obedient to the request from Iris, he rose and went to the piano and began to play while she stood by him, smiling, admiring, emphasising the long intimacy of friendship. Miranda put down the magazine and turned to talk to the hovering Henry Tremayne with smiling and animated encouragement. Paul's readiness to respond to the slightest of smiles, the lightest of remarks, where Iris Woodley was concerned dealt blow after blow to her heart but she did not mean to betray it. She was aware that Iris was a clever woman whose subtle strategies only emphasised her own clumsiness in handling a difficult, fiercely independent man like Paul. She was too much in love to be clever, she thought bitterly. She was floundering, out of her depth, terrified of losing him and knowing that he was slipping through her fingers because she was desperately trying to hold on to him.

She was hurt and it showed. She resented his careless attitude, his casual behaviour, and it showed.

She disliked Iris Woodley and saw her as a very real threat and it showed. Brilliant and successful actress who had played many a part with ease, she found it impossible to pretend that she did not care. Her hopeless love for him must make her an object of scorn and contempt and her desperate need to be of importance to him must repel the man who was determined to keep their relationship on a light and impermanent basis. She wanted to spend the rest of her life with Paul. He only wished to play a very minor role for a brief time and then—exit a lover!

She wished she had the courage to walk out of his life. But she could not run the risk of discovering that he did not even miss her! While he continued to want her, however carelessly, she would cling to that small comfort and try to live with the pain of his ruthless disregard for her feelings.

But, nevertheless, when she went to bed later that night, she bolted the communicating door against him. She loved him but a vestige of pride still remained. He had spent too much of his time with Iris that evening, too little with her, and the dragging hours had been filled with humiliation that even his embrace could not erase.

Very tired, she slept deeply. But not before she had the satisfaction, if such it was, of knowing that he had tried the door and softly called her name . . .

CHAPTER ELEVEN

Miranda stood at the head of the cliffs, her curling auburn hair lifting slightly in the soft breeze. The bright yellow of her dress was a splash of colour against the skyline, attracting attention.

But the toy-like figures on the beach below seemed unaware of anything but themselves. Paul and Iris were at the water's edge, skimming stones across the surface of the sea like a couple of children. The drift of their laughter was carried on the breeze and her heart swelled with bitterness.

Coming to Cornwall had promised so much and disappointed her so greatly. If only Paul had continued to be attentive, ardent, aware of her above everyone and everything else as in those first days at Penmawr, Miranda could not have asked for anything more. But it seemed that he was too proud to give the impression that any woman mattered much in his life . . . and she was certainly too proud to accept relegation without protest. Protesting, too hurt and dismayed to realise the risk to their precarious relationship, she had lost him.

He had not spoken to her that morning. She had gone down rather later than usual and found everyone at breakfast. As she entered, Paul had excused himself and risen and walked pointedly from the room, acknowledging her with only the briefest of nods and the coldest of glances. Pride had prevented her from hurrying after him. Smiling, head high, she had taken her place at table and managed to swallow some coffee while maintaining a travesty of polite conversation with his friends who tactfully refrained from mentioning Paul to her. She was surprised by such consideration, knowing that she had invited only contempt and censure by her behaviour since their arrival. Either they were very tolerant, easy-going people for the most part or they were sorry for her, she thought wryly.

Deeply humiliated, she escaped as soon as possible. Paul was furious because she had barred him from her room, she realised. He could behave as badly as he pleased and she was supposed to accept, forgive, welcome him to her arms whenever the mood moved him to make love to her! She loved him but she refused to be trampled on! She was better off without him if he was only going to make her so miserable! She had never allowed any man to hurt and humble and humiliate her so and it proved that she had been wise to keep from loving. If only she had continued to be wise!

Paul was missing all morning . . . and so was Iris. Miranda could not doubt that they were together. She lay on a lounger beside the pool with a book, trying not to care and determined to leave Penmawr at the first opportunity. If only she were not so far from London. The nearest station was twelve miles away. Paul would arrange a car for her when he realised that she was determined to go back to town. She doubted if he would raise a finger to keep her at Penmawr. Their lovely holiday had turned into a fiasco.

She scarcely heeded the murmur of lazy conversation among the others until Marian Gilmore made a laughing but meaningful comment on Paul's lengthy absence with the merry widow.

'She means to have him, of course,' Lucilla Tremayne declared lightly.

'She'll never hold him!' That was Ann Madison.

'But she'll have scored over everyone else!' Marian's words were accompanied by a soft, rueful sigh. 'I wish I'd married the Woodley millions. Then Paul might be courting me instead of Iris.'

'He promised Cy that he'd look after Iris, advise her and guard her from fortune-hunters. I don't believe he means to marry her. Paul isn't a marrying man.' It was an almost desperate avowal from Susan Denbigh who had tried and failed to persuade Paul into marriage in the past.

'I wonder if we are all so sure of that.' Lucilla spoke lightly, mockingly . . . and Miranda sensed that the words were meant for her to hear.

Her eyes were closed against the bright sun and she feigned sleep, seething with resentment. These women knew that Paul had brought her to Penmawr as his current mistress. They knew exactly how little importance to attach to her standing. They knew that she had no hope of marrying him if that was her ambition. He was not a constant lover and he did not allow any woman to suppose that she had a permanent place in his life. What a fool she had been to encourage his interest in the first place, to fall into his arms with unseemly eagerness like too many women before her and to have fallen so deeply in love that nothing else mattered. It was not surprising that he backed away from the threat of her love, taking refuge in the company of a woman who was clever enough to convey that she asked and offered nothing but friendship. A man might marry such a woman despite the fact that he cherished his freedom almost to the point of obsession . . .

There was a little stir of movement when the men returned from a gamc of golf. Paul was not with them and there was still no sign of Iris.

Miranda slipped away, recognising Henry's obvious intent to corner her at the first opportunity. She strolled towards the cliff-top and from that vantage point she saw Paul and Iris in obvious enjoyment of each other's company, bearing out the gossip that they meant to make a match of it one day.

Miranda turned, blindly. Loving was agony. She had always known it would tear her to pieces if she was ever stupid enough to surrender to it. But Paul, arrogant, autocratic, cruel and capricious, had walked off with her heart, uncaring. She was utterly in thrall to him. She began to walk back to the house, meaning to pack and telephone for a taxi and leave while everyone was lazing after lunch. She could no longer endure Paul's near-indifference alternated with meaningless moments of passion. She had lost her heart and her self-respect but she still retained her pride!

As Paul and Iris climbed the slope from the beach, he caught sight of bright hair and yellow dress that were unmistakable. Anger rose at the inference that Miranda had been spying on them. She did not trust him out of her sight, obviously—and had no real claim to his loyalty. He was still intent on teaching her a lesson. At the same time, he was prepared to admit that he had been too harsh that morning. He should not have snubbed her so brutally before his friends. She was his guest. Much more important, they were lovers—even if she had foolishly locked him out of her room.

He had spent the morning with Iris rather than run the risk of open confrontation. He fancied that Miranda would thrust a quarrel on him and both might say things to regret.

She was very spoiled, of course. She had been too much admired, too much loved, and it made her careless and capricious. She had become too sure of him during the few days they had shared before the arrival of his friends, he thought wryly. She was taking it for granted that he would forgive anything as had the other men in her life. She had mistaken her man, he thought grimly. He did not forgive so easily. Nor did he allow any woman to assume too great an importance or to blow hot and cold at will . . .

Iris sensed that swift awareness of the woman in the distance. She was annoyed. It had been a pleasant and encouraging interlude and she fancied that Miranda had been temporarily forgotten. They had been so much at ease, so close, so attuned. She knew she could make him happy, hold him to her, give him all that he wanted. For the moment he still regarded her as friend and companion . . . and that was unbearably frustrating. But if Miranda was out of the way he would probably begin to see her in the light of a lover. She was determined to be his wife and she was very sure she could bring it about, given time and opportunity. Everyone declared that Paul was not a marrying man . . . but Cy had been a confirmed bachelor until she made up her mind to marry him!

At the moment, Miranda was pushing Paul

into her arms, dealing with him in an incredibly clumsy fashion. The woman was in love, of course. It was a definite disadvantage. It was the mistake that most of his women made, Iris thought indulgently, knowing that he enjoyed the chase and the conquest but did not want the capture that held him responsible for a woman's happiness.

She had seen unmistakable misery in those sapphire eyes at moments when Miranda thought herself unobserved. Paul was putting her through hell with his careless cruelty. Iris almost felt sorry for her. But anyone who was fool enough to fall passionately in love with Paul Keller must be prepared for heartache and possible heartbreak. Iris was sure that he would never love any woman. Miranda was beautiful, intelligent, attractive—but so had been many of the women that Paul had lightly loved. Iris did not consider her to be a threat . . .

She said lightly, generously: 'Go on if you wish, Paul. I'll make my own way in my own time. I expect Miranda was looking for you and I've monopolised you too much this morning.'

Paul took her hand and drew it firmly into his arm, smiling down at her with warmth, wondering how many women would give a thought to Miranda in like circumstances. It was refreshing to know that Iris would not be offended if he did desert her to hurry after Miranda. But he had not the least intention of doing so. It was not his policy to grant any woman that kind of satisfaction!

'Miranda doesn't expect me to live in her pocket,' he said lightly. 'We understand each other too well for that!' Even as he spoke, he wished wryly that it was the truth.

'I'm afraid that she resents us all very much,' Iris said gently, ruefully. 'Except Henry, perhaps . . . but then she knew him, didn't she? It makes a difference . . .'

He frowned, disliking the inference. 'I don't think it's resentment. Some people take time to be at ease with strangers. And one must make allowances for temperament. Miranda has just finished a difficult part in a disastrous play. She needed this holiday, away from everything and everyone. Maybe it was thoughtless to invite so many people at the same time. I thought it would amuse her but she seems too tired to make the necessary effort. I hope you won't hold it against her.' He tried not to defend her too forcefully.

Iris smiled at him. 'She's special, isn't she, Paul?' Her tone, with its warm understanding, invited him to confide in her.

'Special?'

'More important than the others?' she enlarged carefully. 'You tolerate in Miranda what you most dislike in other women— jealousy, demands, temper, rudeness . . .'

He interrupted, disliking the long list of faults. 'I don't tolerate them at all, Iris. I've taken her to task over them, in fact!'

'You've quarrelled!' she exclaimed regretfully. Paul did not doubt the sincerity of her tone. He might have mistrusted the hint of satisfaction in eyes that were as dark as his own if he had glanced at her in that moment. 'Oh, of course she hates us, Paul! So would I hate anyone who caused me to know the rough edge of your tongue! You never care what you say or do in temper. I really feel for the poor girl!'

He was touched by her compassion, the generous warmth of her concern. 'There's no need,' he said reassuringly. 'We shall kiss and make up, I daresay.'

She knew disappointment at his obvious readiness to do so. But she concealed it. 'You *are* in love with her!' she exclaimed in apparent delight.

He was amused. She was a romantic, he thought indulgently. 'Am I?' he countered lightly.

'Oh, wonderful! It had to happen one day! Well, I hope she doesn't care for you and then you'll be well-served for all the broken hearts you've left behind you!' she said gaily, her tone implying the conviction that any woman he wanted would want him, too!

'I might ask you to marry me on the rebound,' he said, smiling, carrying her hand to his lips. He would not disappoint her by declaring that Miranda had no thought of loving him.

'Not you!' she declared, laughing. 'You'd be too anxious that I might say *yes*! I wouldn't, of course. I don't wish to marry anyone. There'll never be another Cy.' She was suddenly sober, looking up at him with a brave little smile in her eyes. 'I miss him so much, Paul . . . even now.' Her voice broke slightly.

He took her into his arms and held her close, comforting. 'I know . . .' He stroked the black silk cap of her hair, framing the lovely troubled face. 'One day it won't hurt so much, I promise. While it hurts . . . well, I'm here, Iris. Whenever you need me.'

She clung to him. 'You're so good to me, Paul. I don't know what I should do without you.' She kissed his lean cheek, subtly conveying affection and no more while her body clamoured for him . . .

Miranda, looking back for the last time before she took the lower path to the house, saw them in that close embrace and knew that all her happiness, all her hopes, were utterly destroyed . . .

Paul and Iris separated when they arrived at the house. She went to change from shorts and suntop before lunch and Paul decided to go in search of Miranda. It was a rare thing for him to offer an olive-branch. But matters would go from bad to worse if he allowed—and he knew that he did not want to lose her. He was beginning to understand why she had meant so much to Kane and why the actor had been so shattered when she ended that affair. For Miranda bound a man almost against his will with her beauty and charm and fiery passion.

He found her in his study. He did not pause to wonder at her interest in the local telephone directory. 'There you are!' he exclaimed, having searched the house and gardens and only thrown open the door of his study as a last resort. It was his private sanctum and no one entered it but himself. Growing anxious, his tone was sharper than he intended with the relief that she had not flown from Penmawr. She had no real reason to go but women were such damnably unpredictable creatures! 'I've been looking everywhere for you!'

Miranda closed the directory and looked at him coldly. 'And I thought you'd spent the morning searching for pebbles! Plenty of them on the beach, aren't there, Paul?' Her voice was light, dry, but it shook slightly. On the point of telephoning for a taxi, she had hoped to leave without seeing him again. The flippant retort, covering her hurt, did not come easily.

She was pale and her lips were tightly compressed. Paul wished he could believe it was pain rather than pique that shadowed her beautiful face. Studying her, he knew a sudden lurch of his heart. She was temperamental, demanding, very capricious. She was proud, strong-willed, stubborn and fiercely independent. He loved her, very much.

Shaken by the final admission, he held out his hand to her, smiling . . . and his smile was a confession of the neglect for which she had every right to reproach him. 'Come and have some lunch, darling. I guess you didn't have much breakfast.' The tenderness of his tone was an apology, an attempt to heal a ridiculous and quite unnecessary rift in their relationship.

Miranda ignored his hand. The careless emptiness of the endearment struck brutally at her heart. He came to her from another woman's embrace, light of heart, utterly without caring or conscience! She ought to hate him . . .

'I won't bother, Paul,' she said stiffly. 'I'm really not hungry.'

'No?' He dropped his hand, hurt and annoyed that she meant to widen the breach with that deliberate rejection. He had no intention of grovelling. He had humbled himself sufficiently for this woman and it was obvious that she cared little for him. He was thankful that he had not betrayed the emotion which abruptly surged through him. He was the last man in the world to admit to loving a woman who did not want him! 'Well, if you won't join us . . .' He turned towards the door. 'I could eat a horse.'

She said brightly: 'You've been working up an appetite on the beach—for more than your lunch, I daresay.' Carefully she schooled her tone to lightness, tolerant amusement. There was no hint of reproach . . . or the heaviness of her heart.

His dark eyes narrowed abruptly at the mocking implication of the words. They were particularly offensive in view of the fact that his friendship with Iris was utterly untouched by sexual interest on either side. It was a rare relationship and he valued it accordingly. Miranda smirched a warmly sympathetic and understanding woman who was genuinely concerned for her with that suggestion of an intimacy that had never occurred to either of them.

But he did not voice a protest. He did not mean her to suppose that she had scored a point. If she resented his friendship with Iris so much then it would revenge that silly slight if he allowed her to believe that she really did have cause for jealousy!

His smile was slow, mocking, hinting at memories she did not share. 'Iris is a fascinating woman,' he drawled. 'I've got to know her really well since Cy died . . . and I can understand why he thought the world of her. There's something about her . . .' He broke off. 'I can't expect you to appreciate my feeling for her, of course. But you needn't be jealous, darling. She isn't one of my mistresses. Iris is the kind of woman that a man marries, you see.'

She flinched as though he had struck her.

Those light words had been so deliberate, so cruel—putting her firmly in her place. One of his many mistresses. Dismissing all that they had shared as a nothing, forgettable!

'Take care or you'll find yourself at the altar before you know it!' she warned with light, laughing indifference. And her heart was breaking at the very thought.

He smiled. 'I can think of worse fates . . .'

Like spending one's life loving and longing for a woman who had no heart to give, he thought wryly, marvelling that he had fallen at last into the trap he had avoided so carefully. What was it about Miranda that he should want her so much? What power did she possess, of all the women he had known, to bind him with the unbreakable strands of loving?

CHAPTER TWELVE

With defeat staring her in the face, Miranda suddenly rebelled. She had meant to go away, to accept that she had lost Paul to a clever woman, to try to forget him. But abruptly she changed her mind. Why should she give Iris the satisfaction of supposing that she had won! Why should she surrender so tamely to the belief that Paul would never love her? And, most humiliating of all, why should she encourage Paul to suppose that she could not bear the constant proof of his failure to love her?

He did not even suspect her feeling for him, she realised with thankfulness. She had kept their relationship too light and superficial. She had carefully concealed the welling emotion, checked the impulsive words that trembled on her lips when she lay in his arms. She had played it just the way he wanted, in fact.

She decided to stay, to stifle her pride. And she determined to punish him a little. She knew her power over a man. She knew that Paul's passion for her was always just a kiss away. Well, he would be on his knees with wanting before she lay in his arms again. She would not be cheapened by his loveless desire!

She reached to brush his lips lightly with her own, smiling, provocative. 'Don't let her rush you into anything, Paul. I'm not through with you yet,' she murmured softly.

There was warm invitation and subtle reminder in that kiss and the brief, teasing pressure of her body against his own. Paul doubted if she was seriously concerned about his relationship with any woman but herself. He did not think it would matter to Miranda if he married Iris—or anyone else—at some distant date when she had ceased to want him. He thought it very probable that the sensual and utterly amoral Miranda would be in another man's arms before many weeks had passed. She was simply not the type to settle for one man.

For the moment, she wanted him. And desire leaped immediately at the touch of her lips. He wanted her, now and for always. He reached for her, wondering if he would ever understand the quicksilver moods of this beautiful, exciting woman.

Miranda did not allow that kiss to become too insistent. She was not too sure that she could keep her own wanting under control, she thought wryly. So she teased him with light, playful kisses, her tongue flickering lightly about his lips, her slender body half-yielding, half-resistant in his arms—and Paul, realising what she was about and more amused than angry, reined the passion that threatened to consume him.

Miranda slipped from his embrace. 'I'm keeping you from your lunch,' she said carelessly, as though his kiss, his caress, his nearness did not disturb her senses almost unbearably.

'Suddenly I'm not hungry,' he said, a glow of intent in his dark eyes.

'Suddenly I am,' she declared, laughing— and eluded him as he reached for her once more.

It was a very hot afternoon. The whole of the country was enjoying a heat wave, the first of the summer. Miranda joined the party on the terrace after lunch, clad only in the briefest of bikinis. It was too hot to do anything but bask in the sunshine, exchanging lazy conversation. Later they would swim.

Paul welcomed her with a warm smile, a meaningful press of his hand—and then turned promptly to Iris in response to her voice. Swallowing her irritation, Miranda sat down by the wolfish Henry Tremayne and indulged him with a mild flirtation. She did not like the man. But he was harmless and very conveniently to hand. Lucilla took no notice for she was used to her husband's weakness for women and knew just how little importance to attach to it. Henry might flirt but he did not indulge in affairs. Lucilla saw to that in her own inimitable way!

Miranda set out to be pleasant, to charm. But she was careful not to overdo it. She knew how to play a part to perfection. Simply and subtly, she conveyed regret for her prickliness with people whose arrival had caught her at an off-moment when she was tired and temperamental. Now she wished to make friends and hoped she would be forgiven if she had offended. The men were very ready to like her, to forgive, to be charmed by her looks and personality. But men were always easy conquests. Miranda was more concerned with the liking and respect of the women and knew it would be hard-won. But, like most women, they were prepared to pretend and the afternoon passed very pleasantly.

Paul smiled when their eyes met and managed the occasional private word. But he was kept busy. Miranda observed his ready response to Iris Woodley's constant requests for a cold drink, a cushion, a certain magazine, suntan lotion, to turn up the radio, to turn down the radio, to pass her bag, to adjust her lounger, to light her cigarette, another cold drink. She marvelled at his patience, his readiness to dance attendance. Each request was made with the sweetest of smiles and the quiet assumption that no one could object to do her bidding. But Miranda noticed that she did not look to any other man for the many little attentions.

Paul seemed happy to oblige. He was an attentive and considerate host. But no one demanded so much of him as Iris. And Miranda took care to ask nothing at all. She gained a glow of satisfaction from the fact that Paul anticipated and provided her every need without parading the matter.

He was pleased by her good humour. At the same time, he distrusted her sudden change of mood. For the moment she was willing to like and be liked. Briefly she chose to charm—and no one could be more charming, more delightful, more enchanting. His friends visibly warmed to her. It was impossible to guess at her motives and it was dangerous to assume that she wanted to please him, he thought wryly. Miranda pleased no one but herself. If she had cared for his opinion, she would have welcomed his friends and encouraged them to take her to their hearts when they first arrived. She was so indifferent, so careless, so confident that she had been scarcely polite and he did not find it easy to forgive.

He was not a sentimental or a weak man. Loving Miranda, he could still regard her with wholly dispassionate disapproval when she offended. His heart might leap at her loveliness and his blood quicken with longing when she smiled but he retained his cool, clear and somewhat cynical judgment. He loved her but he was too mature and much too wise to endow her with qualities she did not possess. He loved her because of very human failings and not despite them, he knew. He was not an Edward Kane to set her on a pedestal and then grieve when he discovered her feet of clay. Perfection in a woman, even if it was possible, was not desirable for it could only make a man more conscious of his own shortcomings. Miranda was a very human woman, passionate and wilful with something of the wanton in her nature—and she was all the woman that he could ever want!

He was not a man to rush into anything. Loving Miranda, he did not feel impelled to declare the fact. He might never do so. He knew from experience that one immediately felt under an obligation in such circumstances and he would not do that to Miranda. He had always disliked it so much himself and a woman's admission of loving had usually sounded the death-knell of an affair. He suspected that Miranda would react in the same way. She was as restless, as reluctant to be tied, as jealous of her freedom as he had always been.

He knew her so well. He understood her very well. They complemented each other perfectly. For the first time in his life, he was ready to offer marriage—and it was ironic that she was possibly the one woman who would never love him, never marry him . . .

That evening, he knocked lightly on the communicating door between their rooms when she was dressing for dinner. She admitted him with amused surprise. 'Your manners are improving,' she commended. 'You usually walk in at will.'

'And you dislike that?' He sat on the edge of the wide bed, regarding her thoughtfully as she continued to apply make-up to her lovely face.

She wanted to say no, that it made her feel married to him and it was a warm, comforting feeling. But that would have been a betrayal of the wish in her heart and she was even more certain that it would be a mistake to let him know that she loved him. So she merely smiled and picked up a lipstick.

'Is that why you bolted the door?'

A little colour stole into her face. She had known the question was inevitable, had wondered that it took him so long to ask it. She could not think of a satisfactory answer. 'Last night? Oh, I was rather tired,' she said, a little lamely.

'And I'm too demanding?' he smiled but his eyes narrowed. He did not expect her to be evasive, like other women. 'You can always refuse me, Miranda.'

'A lover has no rights . . .'

She spoke softly, a little ruefully, echoing something he had once said. But she was thinking more of herself and how impossible it was for her to demand what he would not or could not give. His love.

Paul stiffened. The hurt of loving caused by careless words, he thought bitterly, understanding as he had never understood in the past. She was putting him in his place, he realised. He was reminded that he was just a lover and not her love. He was warned that she would discard him without regret when another man seemed more attractive. He was told that he must not expect to be of real importance in her life.

'Then I shall have to marry you,' he said in his dry, mocking way—and wondered how she would react if he rephrased the words as a serious proposal. He knew, of course. She was too honest to marry any man without love— and she was too honest to pretend that she loved.

Miranda stared, her heart fluttering wildly.

She could not analyse the expression in his glittering dark eyes. She did not know if he mocked her or proposed to her! He did not mean it, could not mean it, she decided, thankful that she had not been jolted by surprise into betraying how much she wanted him to mean it!

She responded in obviously expected manner. 'You do me too much honour, sir,' she riposted, dropping a mock curtsey. Her tone was heavy with irony. He must not suppose, even for a moment, that she was tempted.

Paul laughed. She was a constant delight to him. It would have been a disappointment if she had reacted in any other way to the light words. She had so much spirit, the lovely Miranda!

He rose and took her hands, smiling into the sapphire eyes. 'May I kiss you, at least?'

It was a soft-spoken request, taking her by surprise. She looked at him, a little amused. 'It's late in the day to stand on ceremony, isn't it? You've always taken what you want without asking,' she reminded him, drily.

'Didn't you just say that I've no rights? That must include kissing you against your will.' But he put an arm about her slender waist and drew her close with sudden intent.

Her heart lurched. Desire swept through her in a moment. 'What makes you think me unwilling?' she murmured, lifting her face for his kiss, her whole body tingling in anticipation of his embrace even while her stubborn spirit remembered the hurt and humiliation and desire for revenge.

Her swift response delighted him, as always. At the same time, he was saddened by her readiness to give everything but her heart. He held her and kissed her and desire leaped between them. But it did not burn with its usual fierce flame for Paul and he found it almost easy to release her, to remind her that they were expected in the dining-room.

Frustrated in her plan to thwart him at the last moment, Miranda was furious—and frightened. Was he tiring of her, after all? Was her power losing its potency? It had to happen, of course. One only had to study his track record! Perhaps she should forget all about revenge and take the little he offered with a thankful heart. She needed to store up memories against a bleak and lonely future!

Suddenly she thought of Edward. Had he loved like this, suffered like this? Had it seemed the end of the world to him to lose his love? She remembered how he had refused to accept, clung to the belief that she loved him still, pleaded with her to go back to him. His total lack of pride had astonished her. Now she could understand. For there was no room for pride in a heart that loved.

Edward had found comfort and consolation with someone else. But perhaps he loved her still. Just as she would love Paul for the rest of her life, come what may. Poor Edward. Dear, loving Edward who had given so much and wanted only to make her happy. It seemed strange to recall that she had left him because he loved her and wished to marry her. She had felt trapped, restless, apprehensive of the future. But she might have been wise to have married him, to have settled for the security of loving that he offered. It was too late now, of course. She sighed. If only one could have a glimpse of the future at times. Less mistakes would be made . . .

That evening, Paul was reassuringly attentive, almost neglecting his friends to stay close to her side. Reward for good behaviour, she decided cynically. But she was grateful. His attitude seemed to underline her standing, precarious though it might be, and it restored her failing confidence in the importance of their relationship to him. He would never commit himself to a lasting love but a woman was secure enough while he continued to want her with that fierce and wholly sensual passion, she thought wryly.

Iris smiled on them indulgently and made no move to detach Paul. She was too clever for that, Miranda decided. She would not show even the smallest twinge of jealousy. She was not likely to admit that she regarded any woman as a rival. That would imply that she wanted Paul for herself and she was not ready to admit the fact. It was amazing how blind a man could be! Paul would be led like a lamb to the slaughter if he did not take care!

Henry Tremayne hovered, snatching the least opportunity when Paul's attention was distracted to continue their flirtation. Miranda, bored and indifferent, humoured him idly, never supposing that he or anyone else could imagine her to be genuinely attracted to the man.

Paul was called away to the telephone, an important call. Seeing that Henry was winding up a conversation with the obvious intention of making a bee-line for her, Miranda slipped through a long window into the garden to escape him.

It was a lovely night, the moon very bright and bathing everything in luminous beauty. Miranda sat on the low wall of the ornamental pool with its cascading fountain and trailed her fingers in the cold water, thinking of Paul and how he had changed her attitudes to love and life. She would marry him tomorrow, she thought wistfully, knowing it would never be. She thought of Penmawr and loved it for its charm and quiet beauty as well as its association with happiness. She had many lovely memories of Paul and Penmawr. Whatever happened, nothing could erase the happiness she had known with him and perhaps that outweighed the heartache she would surely know. One could forget a heartache with the help of time. But one always remembered the magic moments in life.

The moon slipped behind a heavy bank of cloud with surprising swiftness. It was suddenly very dark in the garden. Miranda was touched with an odd chill. She rose to go back to the house—and someone moved behind her and put his arms about her. Very sure it was Paul, heart and mind filled with him, she turned eagerly—and realised her mistake. Henry's fleshy lips stifled her instinctive cry of protest and his determined embrace forced her slender body into close contact with his own.

Past experience warned her not to struggle. Resistance only inflamed ardour. A man's strength was superior to her own at the best of times. So, fighting revulsion, she suffered that kiss, that stifling embrace, and waited for release.

How she would flay him, she thought fiercely . . .

CHAPTER THIRTEEN

For a moment, Paul stood rooted. Fury such as he had never known in all his life consumed him to the point where all madness begins, all reason flees.

He recalled that she and Henry were not strangers and that his friend had been very taken with the beautiful Miranda when they first met. He recalled her strange behaviour of the weekend and found it easy to reconcile it with the arrival of the Tremaynes. Had her resentment been directed against Lucilla, Henry's wife, rather than Iris as he had supposed? He recalled that she had locked him out of her room on the previous night—and now he wondered if she had been lying in Henry's arms when he knocked and called her name and received no reply. He recalled his mistrust of her mood earlier in the day when she had been so lively, so vivacious, so flirtatious—and undeniably provacative in that bikini which left so little to a man's imagination! Had she been casting out lures to the susceptible Henry? His friend was very attractive to women but usually too circumspect to enjoy an affair under his wife's eye. But Miranda was very lovely. He did not doubt that she had fired Henry with her own swiftly-kindled desire so that his friend had thrown all caution to the winds!

He turned on his heel, shaking with fury, a mass of anguished dismay and despair . . . but enough in command of himself to know that he could not confront them, challenge them. A lover has no rights, he reminded himself grimly. Miranda was free to bestow her kisses—and more than her kisses, damn her!—wherever she chose. And he was not Henry's keeper. But he would be sorry for the man if his wife caught him in that passionate embrace with another woman!

He entered his study by the long window that led from the terrace. He could not face anyone for the time being. He must master the anger that still consumed him . . . and come to terms with the realisation that all his loving was wasted on a woman like Miranda.

She had stood so quiescent in that embrace, responding so readily to the passion in that kiss. Just as she had always responded to him. She was so sensual, so easily stirred—and so indifferent to the consideration of anything but her own desires. She was a wanton, he thought bitterly. Any man might be the lover of a woman who was so ruled by the swift flame of her wilful passions.

She loved too lightly to love at all—and he was thankful that he had been jolted out of the foolishly sentimental belief that he loved her! It was the first and last time that he would give way to that kind of weakness!

He poured whiskey into a glass and tossed the searing liquid to the back of his throat, still shaking, still sick with anger and contempt— and quite determined to finish with Miranda. She would leave Penmawr the very next day and never see him again! She would not care, of course. There were Henrys in plenty in this world if her taste ran to the type . . .

Blazing with temper, Miranda told Henry Tremayne exactly what she thought of him, leaving him in absolutely no doubt that any encouragement in her words or behaviour had been unintentional. She did not spare him; all her dislike and disgust pouring out in a torrent of rage.

Taken aback, he stammered an apology. She cut him short. 'I should slap your unattractive face,' she said cuttingly. 'But I couldn't bring myself to touch you—not even with a ten-foot pole!'

Size brushed past him, feeling sick with the revulsion he had aroused with his touch, his closeness. She supposed that another woman might consider him attractive. But for her there could never be any man but Paul . . . not now, not ever!

She needed Paul. She wanted his arms about her, his kiss, to erase the memory of those awful moments in another man's embrace. She felt degraded by the careless assumption that she was any man's merely for the wanting. She desperately needed to be reassured that Paul did not regard her as a casual conquest who did not merit love or respect from a man!

Paul looked round as she entered his study by the open window. His eyes hardened. What the devil did she want with him? Wasn't one man at a time enough for her? Or did she know that he had seen her with Henry and hastened to explain it away? The latter was not likely. Miranda would not feel that she owed him or anyone else an explanation for her behaviour. She was a law unto herself!

She was bright-eyed, tremulous, in a state of excitement. The result of his so-called friend's attentions, he thought savagely. He damned Henry to hell. And he was filled with angry loathing for the woman he had been too ready to love.

Miranda was torn between the need to tell Paul of the beastliness she had just endured and the reluctance to shadow the friendship between the two men. They had known each other a long time. She knew that they were close friends. It might be wiser to say nothing. She owed nothing to Henry Tremayne. But she had dealt with him herself and she did not think he would treat her with anything but careful courtesy in future. Paul would be angry and she did not want to cause a rift between friends. And she suspected that Lucilla Tremayne would be swift to suggest that she had invited Henry's lovemaking. She could not trust Paul not to think so, too!

She hesitated on the threshold of the room. Paul rose from his desk, closing a drawer with a finality that suggested he was on the point of returning to his guests. She smiled at him, moved towards him swiftly, her heart very full in that moment. She loved him so much.

'Darling . . .' she said softly, putting her arms about him, smiling into the dark eyes that looked back with a strange expression in their

155

depths. She was suddenly apprehensive. For he was stiff and unresponsive, holding back, unwilling to embrace her. 'Hold me, Paul,' she said achingly, longing for him to catch her close, to kiss her, to quieten the soaring anxiety in her heart.

His hands clenched by his sides. He was very near to striking her in that moment. He suspected that she was filled with a wanting that Henry had triggered—and turned to him to satisfy the need. Any man, he thought harshly, with contempt. Bitch. Wanton. He was so angry with her—and with himself for loving her, trusting her—that it took every ounce of self-control to keep his temper in check.

He was silent, unmoved by her appeal, rejection in every line of his body. Miranda felt as though she was suffocating as pain seized her heart in a relentless grip and radiated fiercely throughout her entire body. She released him, stepped back slightly. 'What is it? What's wrong?' Her voice was very low.

He found it impossible to challenge her, to demand an explanation. He was much too proud to admit to any woman that he was shattered by her disloyalty. He was much too proud to admit that he could be hurt by loving, humbled by loving.

'I'm not a sex machine,' he drawled mockingly, deliberately. 'It isn't just a matter of pressing the right button, you know. I'm not in the mood, Miranda—and this isn't the time or the place. Later, perhaps . . .' His careless tone was offensive.

Dismayed, she put a hand to the back of a chair to steady herself. She had not expected that hurtful rejection, the brusqueness which relegated their relationship so pointedly to the bedroom. She could not believe that she deserved it. Or did he really think that her need of him was entirely sexual?

She smiled, refusing to betray hurt. She said lightly, as he had once said: 'Don't you credit me with any finer feelings?'

'None at all,' he said coolly, striking to hurt.

She was puzzled, afraid. He was suddenly a stranger and she did not know why, how she had offended. 'Then you wouldn't believe me if I said that I love you,' she ventured, her heart racing. She did not dare to allow the intensity of her feelings to colour the words.

'Love is singularly out of place in our relationship, don't you think?' he returned smoothly, furious that she could speak so lightly, so carelessly, of an emotion that had threatened to change his life completely. She knew nothing of loving or she could not joke about it, he thought angrily.

Miranda's slender hands convulsed on the back of the chair. He left her in no doubt where she stood, after all. He was cold, callous, entirely without love for her. She was merely bedworthy—when he was in the mood!

'So I don't love you,' she said brightly,

flippantly. 'Any way you want it, Paul.' Pride compelled the words. She wished she had enough pride to walk out of his life as she ought. But she could not. She loved him too much. She needed him. So she would take anything he cared to hand out as long as they stayed together!

He wanted *out*, he thought savagely. And almost said so. But her lovely eyes were smiling with that dancing delight in their depths that had always enchanted him and he knew that he wanted her still, could not part with her. But he was still angry, white-hot with fury. He might easily say or do something he would regret if she goaded him further.

'Go and join the others. I just want to run through some figures and then I'll be along.' He took a list from a drawer in his desk and began to study it.

'Oh, I think I'll go to bed,' Miranda said abruptly. She hated the contrast between his warm attentiveness of earlier and the cold indifference of the present. She would not be humiliated by his casual manner before his friends any more!

'As you wish.'

With a hand on the door, she paused, hoping for one smile, one word that would make an utter nonsense of the last few minutes. She wondered at his change of mood. Perhaps the telephone call had brought bad news and he was venting his annoyance on her

. . . just as a husband might, she thought wryly. He could not have meant those harsh, spiteful words. He was reputed to be a care-for-nobody but she knew that he could be warm and considerate and caring when he wished. He had reverted to his usual self with the arrival of his friends . . . probably too proud to have it known that a woman could influence his behaviour. When they left, she and Paul would have a few days together before they returned to town and she clung to the belief that all would be well again between them. In the meantime, she would make allowances for a man who was riled by his pride rather than his heart.

Without glancing at her, he said levelly: 'By the way, don't encourage Henry to make love to you. Lucilla doesn't like it.'

She was instantly outraged by the indifferent tone. So he had witnessed her struggling in Henry's arms and done nothing about it! His friends could apparently do no wrong! Or did he imagine that she had enjoyed that loathsome embrace? Totally amoral himself, he probably believed that she was cast in the same mould!

'*You* don't object, I assume,' she said with dangerous sweetness.

'I don't own you,' he returned carelessly. 'As long as you are discreet you may do as you please.'

'Then I will!' she flared—and flounced from

the room, blazing with fury.

In search of Paul, Iris encountered her in the hall. She was unwise enough to ask if Miranda knew where she could find Paul.

She paused in flight. 'You want him, do you?' she challenged hotly. 'Well, you may have him—and I wish you joy! But it's more likely to be sheer bloody hell with a man who doesn't give a damn for anyone but himself!'

Iris looked after the angry girl, a faint glow of triumph in the dark eyes. But there was no sign of it as she turned to Paul, brought from the study by the sound of Miranda's voice raised in anger against someone other than himself.

He said her name sharply but Miranda, halfway up the wide staircase, took no notice. A moment later, the door of her room closed with a bang. Paul frowned, surprised that he had roused her to anger when he had been trying so hard to be civilised.

'I seem to have said the wrong thing,' Iris said ruefully.

His eyes narrowed. 'That isn't difficult,' he said grimly. 'I do it all the time.'

'She does seem to have a temper.' She smiled at him with warm understanding. 'I think I caught the tail end of your quarrel. No harm done, Paul. But what was it all about?'

'Nothing very much,' he said, almost curtly. He knew her concern to be genuine but it was impossible to confide his pain and

160

disappointment to anyone, even the warmly sympathetic Iris. 'A show of temperament, that's all.'

'Still making allowances, Paul?' She was shaken by something she saw in his eyes . . . a brief glimmer of sadness. In that moment, she conceded defeat and was thankful that she had never been fool enough to love him. She had always known that one day he would meet a woman who would humble his heart and it seemed that Miranda had succeeded where all the others had failed. 'You must care a great deal . . .'

'Yes,' he said abruptly. 'I do.' He took her arm and guided her towards the sitting-room and the rest of the party. He spent a few minutes in ensuring that everyone was suitably entertained and would not miss him and then he slipped away and mounted the stairs two at a time.

He expected the door to be locked but it opened at a touch. Miranda did not look at him as she whisked dresses out of a wardrobe and into a case in an angry whirlwind of packing.

He closed the door, leaned against it, watched her for a few moments without speaking. She ignored him, continuing to pack.

'Childish,' he drawled at last.

Her chin tilted. 'Do you think so?'

'It's an empty gesture. You know that you can't walk out of the house at this hour. Or do

161

you mean to sit on a railway bench all night—after you've walked the twelve miles to the station!'

'I can leave first thing in the morning,' she said stonily.

'Certainly—if you still wish to do so,' he agreed smoothly. 'But there's no need to crush everything in cases overnight. Pack in the morning.'

'I prefer to do it now.' She opened another case, scooped armfuls of lingerie from a drawer. The bright flame of temper was dying down but resolution remained. She would not stay a moment longer than necessary. It was finished!

'You will apologise to Iris before you leave, of course.' He spoke lightly but with cold and implacable command.

'I'm damned if I will!' she flared. Then her innate fairness struggled to the surface, quenching resentment of the woman who seemed to mean more to him than she did. Her hands were suddenly stilled in the task of cramming clothes into the case. 'Yes. I shouldn't have dragged her into our quarrel,' she admitted ruefully.

Paul warmed to her. She was passionate, wilful, temperamental. She took life and love much too lightly. But there was a deal of good in her—and one of the best things was her unfailing honesty.

But he was not yet prepared to forgive and

forget. There was no hint of regret or apology for that encouragement of Henry's attentions that had led to an embrace in the moonlight. Did she really think that he was unaffected by her behaviour, that he could not be hurt or displeased by her casual interest in another man?

He raised an eyebrow. 'Quarrel?' he echoed in his cool, mocking way. 'I don't quarrel with my women, Miranda. I kiss them goodbye before we reach that stage.'

Anger rose that he lumped her once again with the women of the past. 'Well, this is one woman who means to kiss *you* goodbye!' she said swiftly.

He smiled, refusing to betray dismay. 'I won't lift a finger to keep you,' he said lightly. He meant it. Love her, want her, need her though he might, she must be free to go or stay as she chose. His kind of loving would not bind an unwilling woman. 'Plenty of women in the world,' he added, too proud to admit that he had found the only woman in the world that he would want for the rest of his life.

'Plenty of men, too,' she retorted with spirit. 'I don't have to be hurt by a devil like you!'

The impulsive words were significant. But Paul was not a man to take anything for granted. She might not wish to lose him but that did not mean that she loved him. He thought he knew only too well what bound them . . . and voiced his thoughts, a little drily.

'But you'll put up with the pain for the sake of the pleasure,' he drawled, his dark eyes reminding her of the excitement and ecstacy that they found in each other's arms.

Miranda melted suddenly, loving him, knowing that she needed him, too weak to carry out her proud resolution, after all. She sighed, admitting the truth in his words. But she would have phrased it differently, she thought, knowing she could endure the heartache for the sake of the happiness he gave her in so many ways, despite everything. When she was with him, she was complete, a whole person, fulfilled in mind and heart and body, utterly content. Without him, her life would be a desert without even the hope of an oasis . . .

CHAPTER FOURTEEN

Smiling, a rueful expression touching her lovely face, Miranda held out a hand in open admission of love and need. What part could pride play when love dominated the scene so completely?

He made no move towards her. Troubled, he looked at her with eyes that gave nothing away. He longed so much for her love and all that she could apparently offer was the desire that he could spark so swiftly. Other women had loved him and he had only wanted light-hearted loving. Now he loved with all his heart and soul—and Miranda was as heartwhole as he had always been in the past. It was ironic.

Refusing to be discouraged, she went to him and reached to kiss his lean cheek with tenderness. 'Paul . . .?' She said his name softly, tentatively, with a little yearning. It was a plea for reassurance. She needed one smile, one word to give her hope for a future she would gladly spend with him if he wanted her —on any terms!

Paul construed it differently. Deeply disappointed, anger flooded him that she could stifle her pride so easily for the sake of her body's yearning.

He would not disappoint her, he decided abruptly. Her perfume was teasing his senses. As she moved towards him, the loosely-tied negligee had swung open to reveal the beautiful breasts, the lovely lines of her body, naked beneath the lace. He did not think it was a deliberate lure. She did not need to resort to such. But it was certainly provocative and desire rose suddenly in him like a tidal wave.

'Yes,' he said savagely, knowing he could not resist her appeal to his sensuality, wanting her even while he deplored his need. 'Why not? I chose the role of lover and I'll play it to the end!'

He swept the startled Miranda into his

arms, kissing her roughly and without tenderness, bruising the soft mouth. She murmured a protest that he did not heed. He lifted his head and compelled her gaze, his dark eyes glittering with angry and passionate intent as he thrust the thin negligee from her shoulders.

'Paul . . .!' she said in swift warning, alarmed by the look in his eyes that held no hint of love or even tenderness.

He ignored her, bending his head to kiss the delicious curve of her exposed breast and she put a hand to the dark, thick curls at the nape of his neck as wanting stirred in response to his passion.

The lace gown fell to the floor. He could still catch his breath at beauty that had thrilled him before. Desire leaped. For a moment, he gazed at her with the admiring eye of the connoisseur. Then, suddenly impatient, he caught her into his arms and carried her to the wide bed.

His hands were on her body in urgent caress. His kiss was fierce and insistent, demanding response. The need was great in him and he was forceful, inconsiderate in his impatience. Miranda was not swept on the tide of passion. She suddenly realised how wrong, how hurtful it was to be taken without even a pretence at loving. She was no more to him than a sexual object, she thought in sudden dejection. The chill of knowing that his need of her was only sexual, swiftly stimulated and easily satiated, crept over her and she shrank away from his kiss, his touch, his eager embrace. 'No! No, Paul!' she said sharply. 'I mean it!'

He pulled her back, roughly. He would not be denied now! 'Don't play games . . .!' he told her harshly and kissed her with savage intent.

She resisted him with all her might. She would not be taken without a thought for anything but the slaking of casual desire! She had to be more to him than just another meaningless mistress—or she would settle for nothing at all! And she meant it this time!

She did not underestimate the importance of their sexual rapport but she was desperate to be loved as well as desired. She wanted him to need her as she needed him—and that need transcended the physical and brought an entirely new meaning to living and loving.

Paul was on fire. She was his woman and he meant to have her! She was tense, unyielding, and fury seized him. He had never forced any woman to submit to him. There had never been the need—and where was the need now when he held the woman he loved, the woman he meant to keep close for the rest of his life? She was trying to pull a feminine trick with a stupid resistance that made a mockery of their relationship. Closing his mind to her struggles and his ears to her protests, he used his superior strength to carry her with him to those realms of ecstacy this side of heaven . . . and Miranda, hating her weak and sensual body that responded of its own volition and hating him because he was so utterly ruthless when it came to taking what he wanted, held his spent body in her arms and stroked his dark head as it lay on her breast and knew wave after wave of love for him.

Paul lay very still, very tense. He was deeply disturbed by the force of passion that had swept him beyond the boundary of acceptable behaviour. He had taken her by force—and it was no excuse that her delight had been as great as his own once she accepted the inevitable. It was no excuse that they were already lovers. He had outraged her right to refuse. Guilt lay heavily on him and that ruined the relationship which had been so right for them both. He could never hold her again without remembering, regretting . . .

I love you, he murmured silently, his lips on her soft breast. *I love you—and this is the last time I shall hold you like this, against the heart that learned to love you, close to the body that will always ache for you . . .*

I love you. The words trembled on Miranda's lips, shouting to be spoken. But she held them back. There was no wrong in loving. But it would be wrong, quite unfair, to force her love on a man who did not want it. Perhaps one day things would be different, she thought with the eternal optimism of the lover. For how could there be so much magic, so much ecstacy, so much mutual delight in each other if they were not lovers in mind and heart as well as body? Paul simply needed time to accept, to adjust to the truth of loving, she decided happily.

Reluctantly their bodies drew apart. She clung to him briefly but he did not wish to be held any longer and she released him, understanding.

'I promised to give Michael a game of billiards,' he said wryly, gathering his clothes and moving towards the communicating door between their rooms. 'I imagine he's given me up. But I'd better show my face downstairs once more tonight or be branded as a very odd host.'

She smiled at him. 'I expect everyone knows where you are . . . and why!' she said, no longer troubled by the possible speculation of his friends as to their relationship and how long it was likely to last. She was very sure that she had a future with him . . . and that was all that mattered!

Glowing with content and deliciously sleepy, she snuggled among the pillows to wait for his return. He would come back to her, she knew . . . to hold her tenderly and securely in his arms until morning in the way that she had come to cherish.

She drifted into sleep . . . and the sun was dancing across the bed before she realised that

169

the night was done and she had spent it alone. She choked back her disappointment. Obviously Paul had not wished to disturb her when he finally came to bed . . . and there would be many other nights to lie in his arms.

Bathed and dressed and ready for the new day, she tapped lightly on his door and entered. The bed was empty. It had not even been slept in, she noticed with a little shock of surprise. Perhaps he had been in her bed and she had been sleeping much too deeply to know it . . . and he had risen early without waking her!

She ran down the wide staircase, lithe and lovely in cream slacks and shirt, a matching cream scarf knotted like a bandeau about her glorious hair, loose on her shoulders.

She found Paul on the terrace, formally dressed in clothes that were more suited to a business appointment than another lazy day by the sea. 'Going somewhere?' she asked lightly, raising her face for his kiss.

Paul did not kiss her. He looked down at her for a long moment, unsmiling. 'Yes,' he said brusquely. 'I'm taking you back to town today. Be ready to leave soon after breakfast.'

Her heart plummeted at the look in his eyes, the cold carelessness of his tone. She did not need to ask if it was business that took him to town or simply the sudden desire to be rid of her. 'Why?' she asked involuntarily, painfully. 'Why, Paul . . .?'

'It's the end of the road, Miranda.' He spoke with finality, his tone brooking no argument.

Shocked, shaken, refusing to believe, she stared at him in dismay. It was a joke, of course. A joke in very poor taste . . . not like Paul's subtle sense of humour at all. But he could not be serious!

She managed to find her voice, to challenge him with lightness, even a hint of incredulous amusement. 'Just like that . . . !'

He shrugged. 'That's the way I am,' he said indifferently, his tone implying like it or not. 'Unreliable, unpredictable. You know my reputation.'

'You wave it like a banner,' she said, slowly, too stunned to cry, to protest. She still did not believe that her only hope of real happiness was slipping through her fingers. How was it possible when she loved him so much, knew that they were right for each other! 'How can you be proud of something that labels you as heartless?' she went on carefully, lightly. 'I don't believe in that stupid reputation of yours, Paul. It's a sham, something to hide behind. People might suspect that you *do* have a heart!'

She was so cool, so matter of fact. Tears, protestations might have convinced him that she did care about losing him . . . and he desperately needed to be convinced. As it was, he knew that she had given her body gladly and with delight—and kept her heart. And if he could not have the heart of the woman he loved then he would take nothing at all from her, he had decided during a night when he had walked by the dark tumultuous sea, struggling with guilt and need and depression. He loved too much to be content with the little that she could give . . . and therefore he must put her out of his life and set about forgetting her as quickly as he could.

He laughed . . . a cool, mocking little laugh. 'How like a woman! But I thought I could rely on you not to indulge in silly sentiment, Miranda.'

'Oh, you can!' she said promptly, proudly. 'I know better than to believe you are capable of caring for anyone!'

The words hurt. For she had good reason to believe that he cared for her—if she chose to believe. He had shown that he cared in a hundred ways. No other woman had known such warmth, such tender concern, such tolerance, such readiness to please and be pleased as he had shown to Miranda, loving her long before he knew it. How could she be so blind, so insensitive? He knew, of course. If she had wished him to love her, she would have longed and looked for signs of loving in everything he said and did. But she resisted the very thought of loving and being loved. She was the one without a heart!

'Then we suited each other—while it

lasted,' he said indifferently.

Miranda knew that he could be cold and cruel. But this was too deliberately and unnecessarily hurtful. Why? What was in his mind and heart? What had triggered the sudden wish to end their affair? Her stupid attempt at resistance—or the fact that she had not continued to resist? She had absolutely no way of knowing.

Perhaps it was due to that foolish mention of loving him, turned too late into a joke, combined with the intensity of emotion she had felt when she held him after that passionate act of love. Had he sensed the wealth of loving? Suddenly she was sure that it was so . . . and he was drawing back from all the implications of that threat to his peace of mind, his freedom. Just as she had fled from Edward's love and longing, she thought wryly. She understood—but how it hurt!

'I daresay you know what you want or don't want,' she said carelessly. 'I'm the last person to hold you against your will! To tell the truth, I'll be glad to end it, Paul. I shall know where I am for the first time since we met!' The bright smile concealed her anguish.

It shook him that she could accept so easily. He had not expected tears, reproaches, pleading. But that half-shrug of slim shoulders, the dismissive smile that took so little heed of the happiness they had found together . . . he suddenly knew that he was wise to let her go even though he felt that part of him went with her. For real happiness could never be found with a woman who was so incapable of loving him.

He said abruptly: 'I know your passion for honesty so I won't beat about the bush. I'm through with playing the lover, Miranda. I'm going to marry Iris.' It was another decision he had reached during the night. He was tired of the many tempestuous affairs which had culminated in Miranda and the knowledge that his life would never be the same again. He had reached a stage when he felt the need of a stable and lasting relationship with a woman.

He knew that Miranda would not marry him. She valued her freedom too much and she did not love him. She was fiercely independent and she would not admit that she needed any man for her happiness. Whereas Iris was lonely and lost without Cy, the kind of woman who desperately needed the affection and comfort and security to be found in marriage despite her successful career in the fashion world. Iris would marry him once he managed to convince her that he really meant his proposal. They might not love but they were friends and they could no doubt settle down quite happily together . . . and marriage would put an end to his restless search for all that he had found in Miranda. Married, he would discipline his mind and heart and body to forgetting . . .

Miranda felt no shock of surprise. She had half-expected something of the kind. She did not believe him. He merely wished to emphasise his determination to break with her, whatever his reasons, and supposed that she would immediately concede defeat in the face of such a declaration. She hoped he knew what he was about. Or he would find himself married to the widow willy-nilly!

'That seems like a good idea,' she said lightly. 'You need a wife who won't try to clip your wings. Iris won't care how many women you have as long as you go home to her at night like a dutiful husband. She just wants the satisfaction of being your wife, Paul. She won't make any demands on you—and that's just the way you like it. You should be very happy.'

He put his hands on her shoulders and looked into the dark blue eyes that gazed back at him so steadily and with no hint of her innermost feelings. 'No regrets, Miranda . . .'

'No regrets,' she agreed with truth. For how could she regret something that had brought her so much happiness, so many cherished memories? Regrets would come later, she felt . . . when time proved that she could not cease to love him and that no other man in the world could take his place. Then she would surely sigh for the might-have been . . .

CHAPTER FIFTEEN

For several days, Miranda had no heart for anything.

She had no offer of work and she did not go out of her way to look for it. There was no pleasure to be found in a social life that did not contain Paul and so she did not accept or issue any invitations. It seemed that her friends were either curious to hear all the details of her affair with Paul and its abrupt end or else much too tactful in not referring to it at all. Miranda found it painful to talk about him but even more painful to behave as though he had never existed.

She was reminded of him at every turn. She had known him for only a few weeks but the days had been filled with him and now her heart and mind and body grieved for the magic happiness of those days.

She understood and yet she did not understand. She knew what had prompted him to end their relationship but she did not know why he had felt compelled to end it so abruptly.

Mostly she stayed home, fretting, praying for the telephone to ring and his deep voice to sound in her ear when she lifted the receiver. Sometimes she wandered aimlessly around the streets of Soho supposedly shopping but in truth hoping for just one glimpse of Paul or a seemingly chance encounter. She knew most of his haunts and some of his rather doubtful business acquaintances. But she had no way of knowing if he had returned to town or if he was still at Penmawr with the lovely, scheming widow.

She dreaded a meeting almost as much as she longed and angled for it. For she would not know what to say to him except that she loved him, missed him—and Paul would not want to hear those things. He had cut her out of his life with abrupt finality and she suspected that she would not see or hear from him again except by chance. She had committed the unforgivable sin of loving him, she thought unhappily, very sure why he had suddenly wished to be free of her in that unexpected and surely undeserved manner.

He had insisted on bringing her back to London, returning her to the very door of her flat in a way that made Miranda feel like goods on approval that had been found wanting. It had been a difficult journey, one she would remember for the rest of her life. Because he did not know and must not know and would not wish to know that her heart was breaking, she had given the most brilliant performance of her career and did not doubt that he had been completely deceived by her lightness of manner.

They had parted on the easiest of terms.

There had been no goodbyes. Nothing was said to emphasise the finality of the moment. Paul had kissed her lightly and walked towards the waiting lift as if he meant to be back the next day or the day after at the latest. And she had blown him a smiling kiss from the tips of her fingers as the lift doors closed, sweeping him from sight. Then she had closed the door of the flat and busied herself with unpacking her cases in a disbelieving dream. It had seemed so impossible that he did not want her any more, that he could walk out of her life without regret, that she would probably never know the touch of his lips or the strength of his arms about her any more.

The days passed and somehow Miranda struggled through them, living only for a ring at the doorbell, the peal of the telephone, the arrival of a letter even though she knew in her heart that it was foolish to hope, to wait, to yearn. Paul was so hard, so determined. Even if it was possible for a woman to soften and humble him, she was obviously not that woman. He was capable of forgetting, of living his life without her. She had meant no more to him than any of those other women in the past, after all. It was just as though their affair had never happened and Miranda marvelled that he could wipe the slate clean so easily when her every waking moment was filled with thoughts of him . . . and many of her dreams, too.

She did not shed a single tear in all those empty days. But deep down she did not cease to weep for the loveliness and the loss, the flame and the futility, the magic and the misery of loving a man who had found it impossible to love her.

One morning she opened a newspaper at breakfast and was surprised by the announcement that Edward was married. Very suddenly, he had married Julia Cloud and a delighted press had seized on the happy event and blazoned it across the middle pages together with photographs.

Looking at the smiling faces, seeing the radiant happiness captured by the camera, Miranda remembered too vividly that day at the *Caprice* when she had seen Edward and Julia together for the first time. She had attached little importance to that friendship. Now they were married—and because she was lonely and unhappy she felt a twinge of regret. She should have married Edward when he wanted it so much. Now it was too late. She had lost not only Paul but also a man who had truly cared for her.

Studying the sweet prettiness of Edward's bride, Miranda remembered even more vividly the warmth of Paul's greeting for Julia at the *Caprice*. He had kissed the girl with unmistakable affection. His voice had softened when he spoke to her. There had been a certain look in his dark eyes, a certain smile that expressed warm and tender liking. And he had put a hand briefly on her shoulder as though he needed very much to touch her. Perhaps he was in love with Julia Cloud. Perhaps he was a man without a heart because he had given it to that girl long before she met him, Miranda thought bleakly. Perhaps Julia was his ideal of all that a woman should be. Obviously the girl had something that appealed strongly to a man. Paul was fond of her—and Edward had married her.

She did not marvel so much at the last. Some men ran headlong towards marriage. Others, like Paul, resisted it with all their might and then fell, all unsuspecting, into the traps laid for them by the Iris Woodleys of this world!

Miranda did not believe that he meant to marry Iris. She could not afford to believe it. It hurt too much to wonder if he found in Iris what every other woman, including herself, had failed to offer! But it caused her some anxiety, gazing at the picture of Julia Kane nee Cloud, to recognise a certain likeness between the bride and the merry widow. It was not in looks so much as type, she decided. She doubted if Julia had the cunning and the shrewdness of the older woman. But there was a melting softness, a hint of vulnerability, an air of fragility and helplessness and feminine sweetness that must inevitably appeal . . . and both women had it in full measure.

Miranda knew that she was a very different type of woman. For one thing, she would scorn to seem incapable of looking after herself or managing her own affairs. No doubt she was too proud, too fiercely independent—and while she was not hardened by experience of the world she had learned to protect her sensitivity with a veneer of casual, careless sophistication. A much younger Miranda had been too impulsively generous with her affections and learned the hard way to take time in bestowing her heart and to be really sure of what she wanted. Better to be thought fickle than foolish, she had decided—and held on to her heart with both hands until she met Paul.

She suspected that all the women in his life had been much like herself. Sophisticated, superficial, light-hearted, playing the game of love with experienced ease, giving little and asking little. But perhaps in his heart he had always wanted someone like Julia—or Iris. Sweet, clinging, very feminine, wholly dependent on him for happiness and security. The kind of woman that Miranda was not and never could be. She did not despise the type. Deep down, she envied her for she knew that such a woman could satisfy a man's every need and boast of a faithful and loving husband through a lifetime of marriage.

If Paul ever married at all, it was very likely that he would marry just such a woman rather than someone like herself. So there was absolutely no point in hoping and moping any longer, she told herself with sudden impatience for the wasted days. The need for Paul would always be with her and she must learn to live with it. In the meantime, she must pick up the pieces of her life. She reminded herself that it had been very much worse for Edward after living with her for six months. He had survived and found happiness with someone else. She had known Paul for only a few weeks and it was not the end of the world because he did not love her. There was more to living than loving!

That morning, she rang her agent and then a girlfriend and set about making a new life for herself in which Paul did not play any part at all. After all, a few weeks before she had not even known that he existed and she had been happy enough!

She went out early and was away from the flat all day, returning only to change for dinner with an old flame she had met when lunching with her girlfriend.

It was very late when she came home, having enjoyed the evening with Michael Powell more than she had thought possible. Tired and just a little light-headed from too many Martinis, she refused to think about Paul as she slipped into sleep. But she dreamed of him . . .

They were at Penmawr and they walked in

the garden, hand in hand. He loved her and she was happy and sure that they would never be separated again. It was a lovely night and the sun was shining and Iris smiled indulgently from the middle of the ornamental pool and Miranda thought how strange it was that she had been afraid of a cold and unfeeling statue.

Paul kissed her and turned into Henry Tremayne. Paul was swimming in the pool and pretending not to notice her struggles. The smiling statue was holding out her arms to him. The garden dissolved in the abrupt way of dreams and she was in bed with Henry while Paul hammered on the door, calling her name . . . Julia, Julia! She was frightened and she needed Paul and the door wasn't locked but when she told him so no sound would come and Henry's loose wet mouth was forcing her against the pillows and Paul didn't care and wouldn't rescue her and kept knocking and knocking on an open door . . .

Miranda woke with a start to realise that someone was hammering on the front door in earnest. Dream and reality had blended so well that she was confused, believing for a moment that she was at Penmawr. Had she forgotten to unbolt the communicating door? Then she sat up suddenly and looked at the small bedside clock, fully awake. It was nearly four o'clock in the morning. Not a conventional hour for callers. But some of her friends were far from conventional, she remembered wryly, reaching for her robe.

Cautiously, she called: 'Who is it?' She wondered why her visitor had not rung the bell. That would have roused her immediately.

'Come on, woman . . . open up!'

It was Paul. Very drunk and not giving a damn for the fact that he had brought her neighbours from their beds. Hastily she apologised and assured them that all was well and then dragged Paul into the flat, closing the door.

He leaned against the wall, hair and clothes dishevelled, tie missing, scarcely able to stand. She no longer wondered that he had not rung the bell. She doubted if he could have seen the bell-push!

'Where the hell've you been? Been ringing you all day,' he complained, his knees starting to sag. His eyes were half-closed, his mouth slack. She had never seen him look less attractive. She had never loved him more.

Half-supporting him, half-dragging him, she got him into the bedroom and he fell across the bed. She pulled off his shoes and managed to coax him into a more comfortable position. She drew the blankets over him, smoothed the heavy lock of dark hair from his brow and bent to kiss him. A blissful smile wreathed his sensual lips. 'Goo'night, darling . . .' he said, turned over and was immediately asleep.

Miranda was wide-awake. She went quietly from the room and made herself some tea. She sat by the window in the sitting-room, drinking it, watching London slowly come to life with the new dawn.

She was very happy. Paul had come to her. It did not matter that he had probably been too drunk to know what he was doing. He had found his way to her. She wondered if he had been driving in that condition and decided he was reckless enough for anything.

He had telephoned her, too. Ironic that she should have waited so many days for his call only for him to ring on the very first day that she was out for hours! But it did not matter. Nothing mattered but that Paul wanted her, came to her . . . and she did not care what had prompted him!

The sun was high when Paul woke. He stirred, opened his eyes, closed them again, wincing. The sun, even through drawn curtains, was too bright.

He had only the haziest memory of the night, following the frustration of the day. He had telephoned, called at the flat, looked for Miranda in a dozen likely places, contacted various of her friends without success. And he needed so much to see her.

He had tried to forget but she was wholly unforgettable. She haunted him by day and night. The sun and the moon mocked the man who found that life was empty and pointless without Miranda to share it with him. Penmawr was an empty shell, echoing with memories of her loveliness and laughter.

He had returned to London, to the house in Belgravia. Miranda was there, too. A scarf she had forgotten still carried a trace of her perfume. A photograph he had taken one day was in the drawer of his desk, her beautiful hair windblown across her laughing face and her eyes smiling directly at him in a way that caused his heart to contract. He could not sit at the piano without recalling the day when they had played Chopsticks together. He could not play a record or pick up a book without remembering their mutual taste in music and literature. And each time he switched on the television set he seemed to tune into a play that reminded him too vividly of Miranda's work in the theatre.

His days were busy for he had much to do to catch up on affairs that had been neglected during his absence from town. But for the first time a woman disturbed his concentration and affected his aptitude.

He missed her very much. His heart and mind and body ached for her and he fancied that he saw her a dozen times a day as he drove around town, frequented restaurants, visited nightclubs and bars and theatres with friends and business associates. He looked for her everywhere, blatantly eavesdropped in the hope of hearing her name on someone's lips— and stubbornly resisted the urge to get in touch with her. She would never give him what

186

he wanted most of all . . . her love.

She had let him walk out of her life with a casual kiss of her fingers. There had been no protest, no pleading, no apparent concern. He had said that he would marry Iris and she had virtually wished him happy!

He had meant to ask Iris to marry him. But the words had stuck in his throat, after all. She deserved better, he had told himself, knowing that the need for Miranda would always be with him.

As the days passed, he discovered that love was a more demanding mistress than any woman, giving him no peace of mind or heart or body by day and night. He also discovered that pride came a poor second to love. He made up his mind to see Miranda, to ask her to marry him. She did not love him but she might be willing to marry him. Without conceit, he knew he was a man that most women would marry without hesitation. He was attractive and wealthy and influential. He could give Miranda anything she wanted and the kind of life that few men could provide.

He spent an entire day in trying to reach Miranda and finally tracked her down at a small restaurant where she was dining with a man he did not recognise. Paul remained in the background with the restauranteur who happened to be a friend. He knew it would not further his cause if he took her escort by the scruff of his neck and threw him forcibly across the room. He must deny himself that pleasure, he thought grimly.

Miranda did not appear to have a care in the world that evening. Paul had expected her to be a little downcast by the news of Kane's marriage for the man had once been her lover and a woman always found it difficult to accept that she could be replaced. Now he wondered if she had a heart at all, the lovely Miranda who had captivated him so completely.

It was a long evening and he was determined not to leave until they did. So he stayed, drinking whiskey with a recklessness that was unusual with him, needing to quench the fire that raged in his blood as she smiled and talked and flirted with the man who might so easily be a new lover.

He had followed the man's car to Seal Court in the early hours, pulled up at a discreet distance and watched them both enter the building. Hating himself for spying on her, knowing it was none of his business if the man stayed the night, he had waited, drinking steadily from a flask. Perhaps he had dozed but he had no recollection of seeing the man leave.

He only knew that he had determined to talk to Miranda without wasting another moment and had marched into the building, exchanging a friendly word with the night porter who knew him well, and taken the lift. He remembered nothing more . . .

CHAPTER SIXTEEN

Paul raised himself on his elbow, very gingerly. Some bloody fool was using his head as an anvil to hammer iron! Cautiously he opened one eye to familiar surroundings and discovered that the faint perfume that had been teasing a tiny corner of his brain was reminiscent of Miranda for the very logical reason that he was in Miranda's bed. He wondered if she had shared it with him and wished bitterly that he could remember more of the previous night.

'Paul . . .'

He turned his head at the sound of her quiet voice, too quickly. Pain shot through his eyes and he groaned. She smiled down on him with warm sympathy and he grinned back at her ruefully. 'Damn you! I've never been so drunk in my life!'

'I've brought you some coffee.'

He swung his feet to the floor. A grimace and another groan betrayed that it had not done him a lot of good to move so suddenly. 'God, I've slept in my clothes,' he discovered with weary distaste. 'I must have been as drunk as a lord.'

'I've never seen a lord in that particular condition, not even Jeremy Landon,' she said lightly. 'So I can't say. But you were certainly very drunk.'

He ran his hands through his dark hair. 'I need a shower . . . and a shave! A fine lover to find in your bed, my poor Miranda,' he said in his mocking way.

She laughed and touched her fingers to the dark stubble on his chin in a light caress. 'It is my bed,' she returned, smiling at him. 'It could so easily be someone else's.'

'Very true.' He drank some coffee without enjoyment. It was very black and very sweet. 'This is a poisonous brew,' he complained.

'Your cure for a headache is much to be preferred, I admit. But I've run out of champagne so you must make do with black coffee,' she said firmly.

'As I remember, there was more to it than champagne,' he said seriously but his eyes held a little laughter. 'No kisses left in the larder, my sweet?'

'I don't know that you deserve kisses,' she said severely. But she leaned to kiss him, nevertheless . . . very tenderly. He made no move to embrace her. He was very still, very tense, and something that was almost a sigh escaped him. 'Now drink your coffee.'

He did so, grimacing. 'My God, you're a bossy-boots. Heaven knows why I want you for a wife,' he grumbled.

Her heart stopped and then soared with joy. 'I can't promise to be a good wife,' she said, smiling. 'I haven't had any practice.'

190

He took her hands and carried them, one after the other, to his lips. 'I expect I shall be a lousy husband. But I'm a fantastic lover if that's any recommendation.'

Laughing, radiant with happiness, she melted into his arms. 'Paul, I do love you,' she said against his lips. 'Just love me and I won't ask for anything else.'

He held her very close, his lips against the bright hair. 'I can't live without you,' he said quietly. 'That's loving, isn't it?'

She nodded. 'That's loving, Paul.' She drew his head down so that their lips met.

They kissed with love, with tenderness. The bright flame of passion would always play an important part in their love story but that kiss set the seal on so much more than light loving. It was the mutual giving of hearts.

We hope you have enjoyed this Large Print book. Other Chivers Press or Thorndike Press Large Print books are available at your library or directly from the publishers.

For more information about current and forthcoming titles, please call or write, without obligation, to:

Chivers Press Limited
Windsor Bridge Road
Bath BA2 3AX
England
Tel. (01225) 335336

OR

Thorndike Press
295 Kennedy Memorial Drive
Waterville
Maine 04901
USA

All our Large Print titles are designed for easy reading, and all our books are made to last.